2/09

OTHER BOOKS BY JEAN FERRIS

Underground

JEAN FERRIS

Underground

Farrar, Straus and Giroux • New York

Library of Congress Cataloging-in-Publication Data

Ferris, Jean, date.

Underground / Jean Ferris.— 1st ed.

p.   cm.

Summary: In 1839, Charlotte Brown is sold north to Kentucky, where she becomes a maid at Mammoth Cave Hotel, falls in love with one of the tour guides there, and gets involved in the Underground Railroad.

ISBN-13: 978-0-374-37243-9

ISBN-10: 0-374-37243-8

1. Mammoth Cave (Ky.)—Juvenile fiction.   [1. Mammoth Cave (Ky.)—Fiction.

2. Caves—Fiction.   3. Slavery—Fiction.   4. Underground railroad—Fiction.

5. Kentucky—History—1792–1865—Fiction.]   I. Title.

PZ7.F4174Und 2007

[Fic]—dc22

2006037385

For Joy Lyons
of the National Park Service,
who showed me the cave,
and
Leslye Lyons,
who showed me the way

Underground

Prologue

I LEARNED TO WRITE A LONG TIME AGO IN A WAY I NEVER could have predicted, but it took me years before I could write down my story of all else that was happening during that time. First I was just too busy to write about it, and I wouldn't have anyway, for fear of being caught out doing something that could have got me hanged, since there were lots of white folks then who didn't want to see slaves learning anything. After that I was too sad to remember it, never mind write it, because it had been a sweet time as well as a dangerous one, and I missed it painfully once it was gone. And then I had another kind of life with somebody who didn't want to know all I'd done, so I tried to put it away. But that time formed me from the sixteen-year-old girl I was into somebody stronger, and braver, and at the same time softer than I'd been before. Now seems like a good time for me to get it down, while it's still all there in my memory and there's nobody left to be hurt by what I want to tell.

1

IT WAS MAY OF 1839 WHEN I GOT SOLD. AGAIN. I'D hardly had time—not quite a year—to get used to the place in Tennessee 'fore the master up and died. I can't say I was sorry, since he was an ugly-spirited man. But the mistress decided to go home to her folks in Alabama, so she sold the whole place—and us, too, just the same as the cows and the chairs.

It felt bad not knowing who'd bought me—somebody in Kentucky was all I knew. But not so bad as the time before, in North Carolina, when my whole family got separated and sold. Mama was first, and then Sally—even though we had our fights, she was still my little sister—and then my brothers, William and Russell. At least the boys got to stay together. But they were going way south—to Georgia, I heard—and that wasn't ever good. I'd never been down there, but other slaves had told me how bad it was with all the heat and the bugs and the working till you just plain fell over. They were big strong boys, but they were only twelve and fourteen years old.

Maybe it was good I never knew what happened to them all. That way I could think they ended up in good places, where they weren't working too hard and there was enough to eat and no whippings. Course, it was hard knowing I most likely wouldn't ever see them again, so I wanted to think good things were happening to them. Or even that they got up the gumption to run and made it all the way north to Canada, a place with no slavery.

It turned out I was the only one sold going to Kentucky, and it was far enough I got to ride in a wagon instead of walking in a coffle. It was a long ride on a bad road with my feet in chains, in the back with the hogs, but that was still better than a coffle.

I was taken to a hotel in the middle of nowhere. And just when I was wondering why anybody would want to come stay there, what with the bad road and the being nowhere, the wagon driver told me I was at the Mammoth Cave Hotel. Before he went off with his hogs—moving slaves around was just another kind of cargo to him—he told me there was a big cave, named Mammoth Cave, somewhere near there, and folks came from a long way to visit it.

All I could see was a square log building, two stories, real plain, that was the hotel, and a lot of trees, so big and full of green leaves I could hardly tell if there was anything else anywhere around there.

The manager, Mr. Miller, came out to collect me from the wagon driver. He called me by my name and told me I'd be a maid for the visitors who came to see the cave. I'd be cleaning rooms, and serving, and taking care of the laundry, all things I'd been doing most of my life and was good at, and some—like setting tables—I liked a lot. He said he'd be watching me close for a few weeks, and if I was a good worker, he'd let me work without a lot of interfering. That sounded good to me. Then he took me for a fast walk around, showing me the kitchen house off by itself behind the hotel building, and the slave cabins arranged in between the trees. But nowhere did I see any big cave.

Then Mr. Miller took me to the cabin where I'd be staying. There were enough slave quarters so nobody had to double up in a cabin. It was the first time I'd ever had a whole room to myself, and I didn't know yet if I was glad of it or if I'd be lonely from it.

After I'd seen my place and left my little bundle there, Mr. Miller took me up to the kitchen house. The cook was a stringy old extra-black lady named Mittie. She had a face like a dried-up apple, and, it seemed, a disposition to match. But she could cook. She sat me down with a mug of cider and a plate of side meat and collards that made me want to be friends with her forever. Course it could have been 'cause I hadn't had a thing to eat for nearly two days.

"That ain't nothin'," she said. "Wait'll you see what I can do when I'm really cookin'. Well, you'll get some of that tonight. We got us a full house of visitors, so soon's you finish eatin', you got to get movin'. I need water hauled from the well and the tables set in the dining room up to the hotel."

Hauling buckets of water from a well is sweaty work, but setting tables, that's a pure pleasure. To this day I love the crisp table-cloths and the shiny spoons and forks and knives, and the plates and glasses, too, even when not everything matches. It all looks so tidy and peaceful and organized, in a way life never seems to be. Even when I knew I'd be the one getting the gravy stains out of the linen and polishing the silverware, I still liked seeing it that way.

I asked Mittie if there were some flowers anywhere to put on the table, and she looked at me like my hair was on fire. But then she told me where there were some wildflowers, and I went and picked a bunch. And greenery, too—the flowers by themselves seemed too little. I fixed them in tall drinking glasses 'cause there weren't any vases like at my last place, and I put them out on the tables.

Then Mittie sent me to clean up, since Mr. Miller wanted a presentable person for the serving. She gave me a jug of hot water from the kettle on the hob, a rag to wash with, and a clean white apron.

Back in my cabin, all alone, the hot water sure felt good. It wasn't always that you got to wash up at all, especially with hot water. I smoothed my hair and put on my one other dress and the apron and went back up to the kitchen house.

2

THERE WERE TWO YOUNG BLACK MEN, LOOKING CLOSE to my age, sitting at the kitchen table with mugs in front of them. A lot about their faces looked alike—enough for brothers, but not for twins.

"Are you two brothers?" I asked.

Both of them stood up for me. That wasn't something that happened too often. In fact, I could say it had never happened to me before.

Mittie said, "You can just ignore them two. They's guides for the cave. That one's Mat"—she pointed to the thinner one—"and that one's Nick. And you two can sit down now and quit actin' all big. They's brothers, for sure. From Nashville. Leased by Mr. Gorin and trained by Stephen."

"Who's Mr. Gorin?" I asked. "And who's Stephen?"

The one called Nick laughed. "Mr. Gorin, he's the one owns everything here, including you. Except for what's just leased, which is me and Mat. Mr. Gorin needs more help here and our master's got too much in Nashville. So he's making money off us, and we get to do some interesting work. Say, what should we call you, anyway? You got a name?"

"Course I got a name. Doesn't everybody?" He might have been gentleman enough to stand up for me, but I could see he had some sass in him, too.

Nick shrugged. "Once I knew a kid called Fourteen. I guess his mama ran out of ideas by the time he came along. Still, I suppose that's a name."

"Well, mine's Charlotte. My mama had plenty of ideas."

"All right, then, Miss Charlotte. Glad to have you here. Improves the view by a lot, right, Mat?"

Mat nodded and said, real soft, "Welcome."

Mittie was back to her cooking, but she said, "And Stephen, he the main guide here though he ain't but eighteen. He come with Mr. Gorin last spring when he bought the cave. Me, I been here a long time. Just keep gettin' sold along with the property every time somebody new buys it."

"So have you and Mat been here awhile?" I asked.

Nick laughed again. He seemed to think lots of things I said were funny that I didn't. "Mat and me, we got here just a couple of months ahead of you. Stephen, he's been here a year. Miss Mittie, of course, has been here forever and knows everything about this place."

Just then the door opened and another black man came in. Not so black as Mittie, but not so light as me. In between. He looked to be older than me, but not by much. Not as good-looking as Nick, but nice-appearing. And ever so neat, which was something I always liked, like he took pains about himself. But most of all, he seemed . . . well, I don't know how to tell it even now . . . like he was *sure* about things. That he understood things, and would know what to do, whatever it was that needed doing. All that, just by the way he was standing there.

Then he said, "Who's this, now?" and he smiled over at me.

I couldn't help smiling back. "Charlotte," I told him. "Charlotte Brown. I'm a new maid."

"You're *the* maid," Mittie said, stirring hard at a pot of something. "Ain't no others. In fact, everybody who's doing the work around here is in this room right now."

So then I knew that fellow must be Stephen and the five of us were all the workers there were. That was a big change for me. Before, in Tennessee and in North Carolina, there had been lots more of us to share the work, and everything else, good and bad, that went with a lot of people living close together. Now I had just these four others, and it didn't feel like enough.

Mittie started laying pieces of fried chicken out on platters. "Here," she said. "Time to start takin' food up to the dinin' room." She put the platters on big trays along with bowls of potatoes and yams and greens and bread. Stephen and Mat and Nick and I carried them up to the dining room and laid them out on the serving buffet. I was glad for the help. That tray was heavy, and the path up to the dining room went a little bit uphill. Four tables of white people were hungry and waiting. I served up the food to each plate as quick as I could while Stephen, Mat, and Nick put out pitchers of water, beer, and cider on the tables.

They left, and I was alone during a slow time while the guests were eating: just a few calls for more of this or that, and I kept their glasses filled up. You never could know how strange white folks would treat you, so I was quiet and careful and mindful, but mostly they just ignored me, which was fine. Then I cleared and I brought up the pies and the coffee and the tea and kept an eye on things till they were all finished and went off for their smokes or their walks or whatever. I cleared again and bundled up the linens for washing the next day. They needed it.

When I went back to the kitchen house to get on with the washing up, Nick and Mat and Stephen were still there, doing that. It was the first time I'd ever seen men drying dishes in a kitchen, but with just five of us to do the work, I guess we had to help each other out.

"You got some good workers here, Mittie," I told her.

"Humph," she said, up to her elbows in soapy water. "Usually they're in a bigger hurry to get finished and get out of here. They was just going slow and waitin' for you."

"Me? Why?"

The three of them were suddenly preoccupied with putting dishes away. "I'm guessing they wanted another look at you. I got that right, boys?" She turned her head and eyed them.

Mat, smiling, took up another handful of silverware to dry. But Nick laughed and gave me a big grin, and said, "Didn't I say the view was improving? Why shouldn't we enjoy it?"

"We don't mean to be uncourteous," Stephen said. "We're just wanting to welcome you in."

I liked what he said about being uncourteous. "I thank you all for the welcome."

"Where are you coming from?" Nick asked.

"Tennessee. It was a big farm, but I worked in the house. The master up and died a little while after I got there, and the mistress sold everything off, including me. Before that I was a long time in North Carolina. Another big place, where my mama and my sister and brothers were sold off before I got bought by the Tennessee folks. Couple more places before that. You two brothers are lucky you're still together." Telling about what had happened to Mama and Sally and the boys made me feel the sorrow all over again, as fresh as new.

"Amen to that," Mat said in his soft voice. I got the feeling he didn't say much, but when he did, it was worth hearing.

"Stephen, he's got a brother at Mr. Gorin's place in Glasgow, just eighteen miles from here," Nick said.

"That's right," Stephen said. "And a mama, too. And Mr. Gorin wouldn't ever sell any of us, so I'll always know where they are."

I knew he was wrong. You couldn't ever be sure you wouldn't be sold. But it wouldn't have been right to say that to him, so I just said, "It's good you can know that. I don't know where mine all went. They're just gone." My voice made a funny little wobble when I said that, one that surprised me much as it did everybody else.

Mittie shook her head. "What's worse than that? Separatin' families like they got no feelin's for each other. Like they won't be missin' each other till forever."

I was afraid to say any more because I could still feel that wobble waiting in my throat. But Mittie had said it right. Till forever.

"Good company helps," Stephen said. "Even if it means we've got to help with the kitchen work."

That made me smile, and everybody else, too. So together we laid the tables for breakfast up in the dining room and then went off to our cabins. Walking along in the dark with all of them was nice. I wished they were still with me when I shut the door and got ready to spend the first night of my life in a cabin by myself.

3

THE DAYS FELL DOWN INTO A PATTERN OF SEEING TO THE visitors, and cleaning up after them, and helping Mittie in the kitchen house.

I finally got to meet Mr. Gorin, my owner. He wasn't around much 'cause he was a lawyer in Glasgow and that's where he spent most of his time. The cave was a side business for him, Mittie said. He left most everything to Mr. Miller, who was true to his word and kept a pretty loose hold on us.

Mat and Nick and Stephen popped in and out doing chores between their time in the cave, which, it turned out, was farther down the hill, with an opening like a giant dark mouth.

Stephen may have been at the cave for only a year, but he seemed to have known it forever. He'd trained Mat and Nick to be guides like he was, and he'd rubbed some of his curiosity and his interest and his enthusiasm for it off onto them. Especially Nick. He and Stephen both loved taking people down there, underground, and they talked about that cave all the time, saying how big and grand it was.

Mat just said, "You should see it."

But that was the last thing I wanted to do. I'd never been inside a cave in my life, and I couldn't see any reason to get started.

My thinking was we all get to spend long enough under the ground once we're dead. Why start any sooner? I couldn't think of anything down there that'd be good enough to make me want to see it.

Mittie, she was the same way. Had no interest in going in there, though she had a respect for everything she'd heard about it, and an opinion about it, the way she had an opinion about almost everything.

"Goin' in there to gawk, that's not the best reason. That cave, it's a serious place meant for serious things."

"What kinds of serious things?" I asked her. "And how do you know that?"

"I been here a long time. I hear things and I think about them, that's how I know," she said curtly. "I just don't want to ever go in there with only one way out."

"There's just one way?" That made me even more sure I wasn't going in there. I was already one kind of trapped. I didn't want to be any other kind.

"Just one way, far's anybody knows."

"I don't like that."

"Me neither."

I sat down in the chair next to hers. Sometimes I just came all over weary, thinking about how my life was. And how it was going to keep being that way with not even one way out. Or just the one—the one that comes at the end. I heaved a big sigh. And then Mittie did something surprising—she put her hand on my knee and said, "I know, sugar. I do know."

4

But avoiding that cave was impossible. Every night, Stephen and Nick sat at the kitchen table talking about the cave while Mat mostly listened. Sometimes we had company with us for our supper: other slaves traveling with their owners. They didn't get to go on the tours, so they were curious about the cave and kept the guides talking. Most of them had never even imagined such a thing as a big underground hole, and they couldn't hear enough about what everybody saw in there.

One thing Nick and Stephen kept telling about was something called Bottomless Pit. They were fascinated with it, and wanted to find a way across it. They wanted to see what was on the other side, though why, I couldn't figure. Wasn't what they had down there already enough?

Nick, he'd say, "Who do you think'll be the first one across Bottomless Pit?" and Stephen, he'd say, "Why, me. No doubts about it." And Nick would laugh, and then Stephen would laugh, too, but not in his eyes. His eyes looked like he was planning something. Mat liked to guide, but he wasn't interested in exploring, the way Nick and Stephen were, which I thought was good. They were enough competition for each other.

One night I'd just gotten all the dishes cleared and the table linens bundled, and was getting ready to help Mittie and the others with the washing up, when this white man came busting in the door of the kitchen house, saying, "Which one of you is Stephen Bishop?"

Stephen and Mat and Nick all looked scared—I knew that look.

Stephen said, "Yes, sir. That's me."

"You're the one who went across Bottomless Pit today with Mr. H. C. Stephenson from Georgetown, Kentucky?"

"Yes, sir."

"Then I want to shake your hand. That was quite a feat."

Nick was looking like he'd been hit on the head with a sack of hammers. Mat looked pretty surprised, too. Not just about Bottomless Pit, but about a white man wanting to shake Stephen's hand. Stephen blinked a couple of times, and then he stuck out his hand, and the white man pumped on it like he was trying to get water to come out.

"That's the only thing Mr. Stephenson could talk about at dinner, how you brought extra lanterns, and how you shimmied across on that ladder—"

I'd been concentrating so hard on my serving I hadn't paid any attention to what the guests were talking about, so I was surprised, too. But I decided from then on I'd do more eavesdropping.

"—and how all those passages go off on the other side of the Pit, completely new territory. I'm Blair Fleming." He was still pumping away on Stephen's hand. "I'm a reporter with the *Ledger-Dispatch* and I want to write an article about what you did."

"Well," Stephen said, and then nothing else. For somebody who always looked like he knew just what to do, he wasn't looking like that right then. "Well," he said again, "as long as it's all right with Mr. Gorin and Mr. Stephenson. They need to know."

"Don't worry about them," Mr. Fleming said, finally letting go of Stephen's hand. "Mr. Stephenson's all for it. And I know I can assure Mr. Gorin it would be good publicity for this place. Can we talk here?"

Stephen didn't need much questioning once he started on his story. Mat and Nick and Mittie and I were all as caught up by it as Mr. Fleming was, though I could see Nick trying not to be.

It turned out that a few nights before, Stephen had taken a long plank of wood from the scrap pile and carried that thing through the cave to Bottomless Pit, his arm near breaking 'cause he had to hold the lantern in his other hand. The way he was telling it, I could almost see it, even though I'd never been in the cave. He made me smell the earthy smells, and see the shadows from the lantern flittering on the rock walls and feel how heavy that plank was while he walked past all those rocky formations and through those big, open, dark places.

Then, when he got there, he let the plank fall across the Pit, not being sure it was long enough to reach to the other side. It was, though barely, and not enough for him to be sure he could go across on it without falling. He was also thinking about how dark it was on the other side since he couldn't carry a lantern while he pulled himself across on the plank. So he had to give up on it that time.

Then, the day before, he got a chance again to go in there by himself, and this time he took a long ladder. Light was still a problem with just the one lantern, but that seemed how it had to be. He laid that ladder across, and it was long enough. Then he set down his lantern and straddled the ladder.

Rung by rung he pulled himself across that pit, not knowing for sure if the ladder would hold, or what he'd be finding on the other side, where it was so dark. "I was thinking," he said, "Nick or Mat might come along one day after I'd been missing for a while and see the ladder and the lantern and figure out that I'd fallen into the Pit. But I got there, to the other side, and I didn't even know I had till my toes hit. Then I had to just sit for a spell catching my breath, and listening to my heart banging away, and knowing I'd have to turn round and go back. But I did and after, I knew it was done. Then, today, Mr. Stephenson showed up and wanted me to take him somewhere nobody else had ever been, and I knew just the place. And we took two lanterns so there'd be light on both sides.

"Still, he wasn't so sure once I pulled that ladder out from a side passage where I'd hidden it and laid it across there. I doused my lantern and carried it over cold, and lit it on the other side.

Then Mr. Stephenson gathered himself up and he came over. We left his lantern lit on the near side. We wandered along a ways, but we could both see there was lots more exploring there than we had time or mind to do, and we wanted to save our energy for getting back. So we crossed over on the ladder again, and that's the story." He shrugged like it was nothing.

They went on talking while I watched Nick trying to get over the idea that Stephen had done what Nick thought *he'd* be the one to do. He took a couple of steps in the direction of the door and then changed his mind. I could almost hear him thinking about how that would look—and how it would make both him and Stephen feel.

As soon as Mr. Fleming left, his notebook full of his scribbling, Nick grabbed Stephen around the neck and nearly knocked him over. "You old scoundrel!" he hollered. "How come you never said one word about that all the while we were sittin' here eatin'?"

Stephen struggled in Nick's clinch, trying to talk. Anybody could see he was all excited about what he'd done, and at the same time, he got how it wasn't so nice to act too big about it.

"What if that Mr. Stephenson wanted to say getting across Bottomless Pit was his idea?" Stephen said while he and Nick kept rassling around. "You think I'd be saying 'No, it was me'? I had to wait till I knew how he was going to tell the story."

"You was lucky," Mittie said. "Lucky with how Mr. Stephenson told it, and lucky you didn't fall in there."

"You're right, Mittie," Stephen said. "And sometimes being lucky is better than being smart."

Mat stepped up and shook Stephen's hand. "I think you're smart, too," he said quietly.

"Thanks, Mat," Stephen said. "Wait'll you see what's on the other side of that pit."

"I'll do that as soon as you build a bridge there."

Stephen laughed.

"You just beat me to it," Nick said. "I thought about usin' that ladder. Then I went lookin' for it and I couldn't find it anywhere. Guess now I know where it went."

I doubt we'll ever know if what Nick said was so, but I liked seeing how Nick and Stephen were with each other. Even though Nick felt showed up, he could make himself be glad for Stephen. And Stephen knew how Nick was feeling, and he wasn't making it worse for him.

Mittie kind of humphed and said, "That cave ain't big enough already, you need to go and make it bigger? You sure you got good sense?" But I knew how everybody really likes being next to something special when it's going on. It doesn't happen so often that you can get too used to it—and I saw how her eyes were watching everything and having that excited shine in them.

We all had to sit down and hear Stephen tell about it again, and Mat and Nick, they had a lot of questions they needed to get answered. Nobody but those three was going to get any words in sideways—lucky Mittie and me didn't have anything to say about it. In fact, Mittie snuck off for her cabin once Stephen started telling his story over *again*.

I thought I was hiding a yawn in back of my hand, but Stephen saw me and laughed. "Guess my audience has heard 'bout enough. Sorry to keep going on."

I was embarrassed, but no matter how exciting what he'd done was, I'd heard that story two times already. I'd been up since dawn and my bed was calling to me.

"Don't mind me," I told him. "It's wonderful what you did. Truly. But my day's been a long one. You three just keep on talking."

Stephen stood up. "I think we all need to be leaving now. The morning comes around fast and we've got to be ready for it."

"Now, don't you go findin' any more new places in there tomorrow," Nick said to Stephen. "Leave some for the rest of us to be heroes about. You hear me?"

Stephen laughed again. He was in a laughing mood, all right.

I was starting to feel in the lucky direction about the place I'd landed. In North Carolina there had been jealousies about who got to work in the big house like Mama and Sally and I did, and there was always the one fellow all the girls wanted, and that caused cat fights. In Tennessee there just wasn't any cooperation. Nobody wanted to help anybody else do anything, and there was lots of blaming, too. Cranky as Mittie might be, quiet as Mat was, here I could tell we were at least trying to keep things smooth for each other.

5

WE ALL FOUR WALKED DOWN THE HILL TOGETHER toward our quarters. Then Nick and Mat stopped at their cabins, and Stephen and I went on a little ways to ours.

"You had yourself quite a day," I said.

"I know I did a hard thing, a thing not everybody could do. And I was scared about it. But it was something I wanted and something I liked doing, so there's that. I know Nick would have made it, too, sooner or later. You think I've got too big a head about it?"

"You ought to have a big head about it. How often does somebody like us get a newspaperman wanting to write about something we've done?"

"That was a queer thing, wasn't it? Here I was thinking Mr. Stephenson was going to be taking the credit for getting across Bottomless Pit and I wouldn't be able to say one thing about it.

What can somebody like us do about it when things don't go our way? So that was an extra thing to be celebrating about."

"Good to celebrate while you can," I told him. "You know how fast things can turn."

"I found out about that when Mr. Gorin bought this place last year and put me here, away from my mama and my brother. Tandy's his name. Now and then Mr. Gorin gives me a pass so I can go see them. But we're not together every day like we were in Glasgow."

"But you know where they are. That's a good thing, believe me, even when I know how you must be missing them."

He looked up at the starry sky and breathed a big deep breath. "This is some kind of life, isn't it?" he said. "Something good happening inside something bad."

"Seems to me you've got more good than a lot of folks." I don't know what I was thinking, to say that to him, seeing as how we both were what we were. But I'd seen how being a field slave like William and Russell were could be a whole lot different from being a house slave, and how Stephen and I really could say we were lucky compared to how it was with my brothers.

I'd heard stories about, and seen with my own eyes, cruel masters, and overseers who liked giving whippings, and not having enough to eat, while here we were sitting pretty in a place where we got good food and lots of it, and nobody was being mean to us. Even our meat came delivered to us already smoked and salted, so we didn't have to be bothered with the butchering, which I always hated.

My last owner—the one that died in Tennessee—was a churchgoing man. He made his family sit at the table every night and listen to him read from his Bible before he'd let them eat. And then he'd turn round and tell his overseer to do things to his slaves that he wouldn't even do to his house dogs, the ones he let sit on his lap and lick him in his face and eat off his plate. And he made sure he hired an overseer who wouldn't even blink an eye at doing those things. Now and then they'd both get upset if they went too far and fixed that slave so he'd never work again—or sometimes never breathe again. But the fault of that was always on the slave, not on them. The slave was weak. Or defying, or too stubborn. Or something else. But it was always his fault. Or hers, sometimes.

"I know I'm lucky," Stephen said to me in a soft voice. "Mama always did tell me that. 'Cause the work I had to do at Mr. Gorin's was work I liked doing. That's still true here. And 'cause the only owner I can remember is one who never raises his hand or his voice. Except once in a while to Tandy. Tandy isn't one to get right at his chores. But 'cause of the way Mr. Gorin is, Tandy never worries about it."

"I'm thinking your mama had another owner besides Mr. Gorin. Am I right?"

"She did. How did you know that?"

"How else would she know how lucky you were unless she had something to measure it against? Did she tell you anything about him?"

Stephen shook his head. "I'm guessing it was bad. But Mama always said we didn't need to know about those things. All we needed to know was that some owners have no hearts and there's nothing you can do about it except to stay out of their way as much as you can. I've heard enough to know some of what can happen. Like I know my daddy, and Tandy's, too, was my mother's owner. And that he sold her to Mr. Gorin before Tandy was born. How many owners you had?"

I thought back, past my Bible-reading owner to the one before him who was flying high for a long while, and then had a big failure of his plantation, so we all had to go. I never did understand about what caused a "business failure"; just that I heard him being called a "broken man." Which was funny when I thought about how many men—and girls, too—he'd *really* broken. Before that, when I was just little, we were on a quiet place I can't remember too much, and there was one before that, where I was born. Where Mama's owner was my papa. And Russell's, too. Just like Stephen and Tandy.

"Four before Mr. Gorin," I told him. "All different, but all the same in the way they thought about us. Like we were only there for the using. Like with your mama, and mine, too."

Something hard or angry must have come into my voice then 'cause I saw Stephen look at me in a different way. I made myself quiet my voice and say, "Four owners, and maybe five, since I don't know about Mr. Gorin yet, thinking me and my folks were just something else to own and use up."

I could feel that thing in my voice again, and I tried to put it away with a deep breath. "It's no good worrying about it, though, is it?" I asked him. "Nothing's going to change. So yes, I think you've been real lucky. You're the least slavelike slave I've ever seen."

Stephen just stood there in front of me, and then he said, "Good night, Charlotte," and went off to his cabin. And I went to mine.

6

THE SUMMER STAYED HOT AND BUSY WITH TOURISTS. Even when we had rain pouring down they came, and went inside the cave, where they said they never could hear the downpour or the thunder and lightning. It was always quiet in there.

And Stephen kept on finding new things. It seemed like he was inside that cave all the time, what with leading his tours and doing his exploring. After he found how to cross Bottomless Pit, Mr. Gorin let him do all the exploring he wanted whenever he had free time, as long as he told Mr. Miller when he was going and a guess of when he'd be back. Mr. Gorin even gave him a compass to take down inside with him, to help him find his way out. Mr. Miller, who, like Mittie, had no intention of ever going into the cave himself, seemed to push Stephen to go farther and search harder for new discoveries. That felt off to me, that someone too fearful to even put his own foot in would encourage someone else to be so bold-spirited. But Mittie, who had seen a lot over all her years of how people behaved, said it was likely all Mr. Miller cared about was having Stephen find more things the tourists would like. And if Stephen did something too risky and got hurt, or worse, well . . . he was only a slave. I doubted Stephen would like thinking that.

Some days Stephen came out of the cave only long enough to eat, or to tell about some new place he'd found—a big dome he named for Mr. Gorin, new passages on the other side of Bottomless Pit, and, most amazing of all, a river! Under our feet as we walked around every day, way deep down underneath us, a river was running!

The day Stephen discovered that was like the Bottomless Pit day, with him sitting at the kitchen table saying nothing about it. But now that I was better at eavesdropping on the visitors' conversations, I heard the talk of it up in the hotel dining room while I was serving.

"Did you hear about what the guide Stephen found today?" a man said at one of the tables.

"You mean the river?" a lady said.

"Imagine! A river under there."

"It's not so surprising," another man said. "After all, the whole cave was formed by water. There had to be some under there somewhere."

I nearly dropped the platter I was carrying. That cave was made by *water*? How could that be? But they kept talking, so I kept listening as I made my way around that table, offering second helpings of cutlets.

"Did you hear what he named the river?" a lady asked.

"Yes," the first man said. "How do you figure he knew a name like that?"

"He said he'd had a visitor earlier in the summer who was a professor of classics," the second man said. "The professor spent a whole tour teaching Stephen Greek words and telling him Greek myths since so many of them have to do with caves."

I never had heard of Greek myths. I thought he was saying "Greek *mists*." I was going to have to ask Stephen about that.

"And rivers. So he named it the river Styx."

Everybody at that table started laughing about that, but I didn't see what was so funny about a river named "Sticks." Because the river Styx was something else I'd never heard of. Another thing to ask Stephen about.

"Did you see that newspaper article about Stephen?" the first man asked. "There are several copies of it in the sitting room. He's quite an explorer. And he's learned a good bit about geology from other visitors. Not that *I* could tell him anything about it." The others at the table laughed.

"Do you think we could get on his tour tomorrow?" the lady asked. "Maybe he's found some other new thing he could show us."

"You'd best arrange it with Mr. Miller right after dinner," the second man said. "I think there'll be quite a few others with the same idea." Then he looked up at me standing there with that platter of cutlets and said in this sharp voice, "We've had all we want." So I had to move on to the next table and not hear more.

After that, I was too rushed, going back and forth between the kitchen house and the dining room, to say anything except, "Stephen, did you find a river down there today?"

He looked up quick from his dinner and said, "They're talking about that in the dining room?"

I heaved the tray onto my shoulder and said, "They're all wanting to be in your tour tomorrow, hoping they'll see something else big and new."

Then I had to go, but not before I saw Nick and Mat looking at Stephen with their eyes wide and surprised.

When I got back, only Mittie was there, starting in on the washing up.

"Those boys, they had to see that river," she said, "so they all gone down into the cave."

"But it'll be dark soon," I said, and then felt stupid. I'd heard enough about the inside of that cave to know that it was always dark in there. A lot more dark than it ever got outside. I expected it was hot in there, too, being so much closer to hell.

"Dark won't bother them none where they're going," she said. "Just hope they ain't disturbing those spirits in there."

"Spirits?" I said. That was the first I'd heard of any spirits in the cave, and just one more reason for me to keep myself up top. Mama used to say there were spirits everywhere—restless souls who couldn't quite make it all the way to the other side for some reason. They've got unfinished business here, or they're curious about how something's going to work out, or they're missing somebody still here too much. But why any spirit would want to hang around under the ground where it's always so dark beats me.

"I heard stories from the miners used to work down inside," Mittie said, "and from some old guides and from a couple of visitors, about how they hear things in there."

"What kind of things?" I asked, imagining chains rattling, and moaning and all.

"Things like footsteps. Sometimes like more than one person walkin'. And whisperin', even if you can't understand the words."

"That's all?" Somehow I felt relieved. Those spirits didn't sound like the dangerous kind—the kind that throws things and makes it cold all around you—the kind Mama knew about. She said she'd seen a few, but I never had, thank the Lord.

"That's all I ever heard about," Mittie said. "Doesn't seem like that cave'd be the best place to haunt. Maybe they're tired, boring old spirits."

I had to giggle. "I was just thinking the same thing—that if I was a spirit, I'd sure pick me a more exciting place."

"This here place now is about the most excitin' I ever seen it in all the years I been here. That newspaper article about Stephen's got lots more people comin' than in any other summer."

"You know what that paper said?"

She gave me one of her narrow-eyed Mittie looks. "You think I can read? You know anybody who can?"

There'd been a slave on the farm in Tennessee who could. A few words—like "Danger," or "Keep Out," or "Whites Only." But reading wasn't something any of us ever got a chance to do, much less learn. Especially since it was against the law. Anyway, we had no books, no newspapers. Mama had a Bible, given her by the mistress in North Carolina, but she couldn't make out one word in it. Still, it gave her pleasure just to have it. I hoped it was still doing that for her.

"No," I told her. "Did you ever want to learn?"

"I heard it ain't against the law here in Kentucky, but still, white folks don't like it, so I don't think about it," she said. "What am I gonna need to read, anyhow?"

I hadn't ever thought about learning to read—and not just 'cause I was afraid. Mostly 'cause, like Mittie, there wasn't anything I *had* to read. Reading had always been such a big mystery to me— big as the stars or the moon—but now that I knew I was in a place where it was legal and all, it came on me all of a sudden that I wanted to learn how to do it—and I didn't have one single idea how I was going to accomplish that.

That night I dreamed I was sitting in a room with a fire going in a fireplace, my chair covered with red velvet like the chairs in my last master's library, and I had a book on my lap. I was sitting in my red velvet chair, warm by my fire, reading a book, just like a free person.

7

WELL, STEPHEN WAS SWAMPED, THAT'S ALL. EVERYBODY wanted to go with him on his tours. Mat didn't seem to mind guiding the extra people, but Nick, he was a different story. He just plain hated it. The ones who wouldn't fit on Stephen's tours were out of humor to begin with, so they weren't the best company, which Mat could handle. But I had to feel a little sorry for Nick, heading off with grumbling people, and him not being in the prettiest mood either.

Stephen was pleased, of course, that so many people wanted to go with him, but also embarrassed about all the fuss. I liked seeing that. Getting a big head isn't a good idea, no matter who you are. You can't ever tell what that can lead up to.

Nick found a new place now and then on his off hours, but I could see it just about killed him doing it. Stephen was curious, that's all. He liked the looking. But Nick didn't really have the knack or the experience. He was just green jealous.

One time Nick was telling me how he had to squeeze himself down through this little hole, trying to see where it went to, and how he got stuck in there for a minute and was figuring he'd come to the end of his days, and I had to say, "You must be crazy. Why do you want to put yourself in that kind of a spot? What good's coming from that?"

He shrugged his shoulders and gave me that smile of his, and said, "How 'bout you let me take you in there, show you around, see why it's such a big thing with these tourists."

"No, sir, thank you very much. No way in the world am I going in there. Not with you, not with nobody. I don't like the dark and I hear that's about all you've got in there. Not to mention those spirits making noises."

"Oh, pshaw. I've never heard a thing in there I couldn't figure out what it was. Anyway, I'd be there with you. What have you got to worry about with Nick by your side?" And he moved over a little closer to me.

I backed up a couple of steps. "Didn't you hear me say no?" I asked him.

"Oh," he said, surprised.

I was thinking Nick didn't get said no to by the girls too much. He must have been used to having more choices than he had there with just me and Mittie. And I knew I'd see what kind of person he was by how he answered me.

He backed up a couple steps himself, then gave me his big old grin and said, "Well, I guess it'll be up to me to change your mind, then. Just you give me some time. I'll have you beggin' to go see that cave with me."

"We'll see about that," I told him. But inside I felt good. He was a gentleman, after all.

Finally it was September, the visitors started slacking off, and we weren't all having to work like there were dogs on our heels.

One Thursday morning at the end of September, Mr. Miller surprised us by coming in when we were all having breakfast, early, before the visitors needed theirs, and he said, "There are only four guests in the hotel today, a family with two young boys. Since the weather's finally turning colder, I think we'll be seeing the end of the season soon. Mr. Gorin should be along in a few days to make arrangements for the winter. Nick, you take the family on their tour. Because of the children, they don't want anything too exciting, so Stephen isn't necessary." I could see how much Nick didn't like hearing that. "The rest of you can take care of things up here, getting the hotel ready for winter." And he started listing things for us to do, while Nick just kept his eyes on his plate.

After Mr. Miller left, I said, "What kind of arrangements for the winter does Mr. Gorin make?"

Mittie took her time chewing on some grits and then said, "I doubt everybody'll be staying here. Usually, me, Mr. Miller, and a guide, in case we do get the out-the-way visitor. That's all we need."

"How many people come in the wintertime?" I asked.

"Not too many. But when they come, they still need cookin',

and guidin', and a place to sleep, and there needs to be somebody here lookin' out for things. But that little bit of work won't take five of us. I'm guessing Mat and Nick will go back to Nashville until next spring when we'll need them again. I'm not sure what Mr. Gorin will do with you, Charlotte."

Mat shot a look at Nick, who still had his eyes on his plate, and now he was shaking his head at his next bad news.

And I was thinking I'd be getting sold again. Where else would I go for the winter if I wasn't here?

8

AFTER I SERVED THE VISITING FAMILY THEIR BREAKFAST, and helped clean up, I watched them go off with Nick to the cave. Then I stood at the kitchen house window looking out at the trees, and the hotel, and the paths, thinking this was the best place I'd ever been, and I was going to miss it. I'd never seriously thought about running before, not even after Mama and Sally and the boys got sold away. I'd seen what happened to the slaves who tried it, both in Tennessee and in North Carolina. One got torn up by dogs, one drowned herself the day after they brought her back, and one got his toes cut off to make sure that was the last time he tried it. One we never saw again, but we didn't know if it was because he got away, or because he got killed trying to. But with maybe getting sold once more as the winter came on, and with my family finished, I started thinking, Why not just go? Why not try to get free so I'd never have to worry about me or anybody I cared about being sold?

Stephen was sitting at the table cleaning lanterns, all spread out on a newspaper, and Mittie, she'd gone off to see to the last of her vegetable garden.

"What are you thinking?" he asked me while I kept looking out the window.

I jumped. He was being so quiet, I'd forgotten he was there. "Oh. Just about where I might be heading next. I hate not knowing what's going to happen."

"You like it here?"

"Best place I've ever been. The work's not too hard, I have good folks to work with, if you don't count how Mittie gets . . ."

He smiled and gave me a nod. "She told me once I should try and stay on her good side, and I asked her if she had one. She threw an apple at me."

I laughed. "I like how no bad things happen to anybody—except for apples getting thrown. I like having my own cabin, too, though that took me some time getting used to. Always before there were others sleeping near me. But now I like having my quiet at day's end."

"Yeah, this is a good place," Stephen said. "At first I didn't want to come here, leaving Tandy and my mama, and now I don't ever want to go. Too much exploring to do yet."

I asked him then if he really thought water made that cave, and he told me yes, that he could see it happening. He saw how the water seeped through little cracks and dripped down, the drips carrying stuff that built up shapes where the water fell. And the drips widened the cracks till they got big enough so the sides fell in, making caverns. He said he would have figured that out just from looking, even if no tourist ever explained it to him. But more than one had. Folks who read about it, and taught it, and understood it. At first it surprised me they'd tell so much to Stephen, but then I thought about how nice it is when somebody is interested, the way Stephen was, in something you know about, and how you just want to tell them everything. And Stephen, he was a big question-asker, which made people want to give him answers.

Maybe he could give me one. "You think I'm gonna get sold?"

He put down his rag. "I don't know why you would. You do good work. They need you here. And I hope not." He gave me a smile so sweet I wanted to save it in a jar to have for later. It was nothing at all like Nick's jokey, cocky ones.

"You do?" Some little catch came into my voice.

"I'd sure miss seeing your pretty face every morning."

"You've been looking at my face?"

"Kind of hard not to when it's what I want to see."

Well, I was plain flabbergasted. I had no idea he was thinking of me like that. And suddenly I remembered I never had asked him about that river Sticks, which gave me something to say when I was feeling so astonished and out of words.

I cleared my throat and said, "I've been meaning to ask you about that river you found."

He blinked at me, surprised-like. I guess he was expecting me to say something different, which I would have if I'd been able to think what it was.

He sighed and said, "Well, what do you want to know about the river?"

"How come you call it 'Sticks' and everybody thinks that's so good?"

"Oh. Well, it's not 'sticks' like little pieces of wood. It's spelled different. The river Styx is the one in the Greek myth that the dead people went across to go to the underworld. 'Cause that's underneath, too, like our cave. I guess that's why people like that name."

"They have to cross over a river in the mist? I never heard of that."

"*Myth,*" he said. "Not 'mist.' A myth is a story." And he dipped his finger in the soot from the lamp and wrote on the newspaper two words. I suppose he meant to show me the difference, but of course I couldn't tell it.

"You can write?" I said in a little whisper. He might have been thinking the cave was a miracle, but I was thinking, This is a slave, writing!

He smudged over the words with the cloth he was cleaning the lamps with. "You never saw that," he said.

"You can write," I whispered again. "How did you learn that? Does anybody else know you can?" I grabbed up a towel and a dish so I'd look like I was doing something besides plain old goggling at him in case somebody came in. But goggling was all I really was doing.

He went back to polishing a lantern. "Mr. Gorin knows. And he doesn't mind. He let me look at his books when he figured out I could read."

"You read, too?" I almost dropped the dish.

He smiled at me, that sweet smile, and said, "You can't write if you can't read. How else are you going to know what you wrote?"

I felt stupid then, but I reckoned he was right.

"Did you read that article in the newspaper about you?"

"Yes," he said, rubbing hard on a lantern. "Sure seemed strange seeing my name in a newspaper."

"How did you learn?"

"I . . . I don't know, to tell the truth. Mama read a little. Mostly recipes. Maybe she just figured it out somehow. I don't know. She showed me what a few words meant, in the recipes. Then I just . . . I can't say . . . I just learned, that's all. I took to saving newspapers Mr. Gorin was throwing away, and I got so I could read them, too."

"You could teach me. You could, couldn't you?"

"Well . . ." He was taking a long time to think it over, and I was scared I'd overstepped.

"Oh, sorry," I said. "I don't mean to—"

Then he said, "We're not supposed to. That's a fact. Mr. Gorin is all right about it with me. He even likes it, how he got this special kind of slave. But he still tells me to be careful who knows, since there are lots of white men, including Mr. Miller, who don't take to it, even in places, like here, where it's not against the law. And he said I shouldn't get any ideas about teaching anybody else."

"You know," I told him, "I get almighty tired of being told what I can do and what I can't, when I can do it and when I can't. Don't you? Especially about things that won't hurt anybody by doing them. Who's going to care if I can read a recipe, or a piece in a newspaper?"

"They think it makes us dangerous," he said. "It makes us think we can be the same as them, not something less, the way they say we are. And once we start thinking that way, we won't be so easy to keep down. That's what it is."

"Well, I already think I'm not something less, even without reading. Being owned, it just makes a pain in my heart all the time."

He reached his hand out like he wanted to touch me, but he didn't.

"Just today, I thought if I was going to get sold again, I might as well try to run away. Getting sold . . . there's nothing worse."

"Would you know where to go?"

"Canada's what I hear. It's better than the free states 'cause even if you get to one of those, the bounty hunters can still catch you and take you back. But I don't know how to get there."

"How do the runners do it?"

I shrugged my shoulders. "I hear they go by the North Star and there're folks along the way who help. Why? You thinking of running?"

"Maybe you'd say it's strange, but I never have thought about it, not for even one minute. Why should I? I have work I like, I have enough to eat. Nobody's doing anything to me. I could be worse off if I ran."

I had to admit to myself maybe he had something there. I

didn't want to even think it, but maybe running wasn't better for everybody. "But being *free*. Doesn't that mean something for you?"

"I feel I *am* free." He started in on another lantern. "Inside that cave I'm *free*. I go where I want. I tell white people what to do, and they do it. I come out when I choose. Nobody's calling me any bad names in there. Might be that's one other reason why I like it so much."

"You can still get sold."

"That won't happen." He said that real strong. "Me and Mama and Tandy will always be with Mr. Gorin."

But he was so wrong. That *could* happen.

I breathed a big sigh. This was all just a lot of talking. I wasn't going anywhere, at least not right away. What I wanted then was to learn to read, and to write my name. I wanted to see how "Charlotte" looked in writing.

"So," I said, "you want to teach me reading and writing, or not?"

He was quiet a minute before he said, "I don't know how good a teacher I can be since I don't know how I learned. And I know Mr. Gorin doesn't want me to. But I can try. We can start right now." He pointed to a word on the newspaper under the lanterns. "That word says 'Man.' You see right there? That's 'M' and it sounds like m-m-m-m."

Just then Mittie came back in, a basket on her arm full of the last vegetables from the garden. "We'll finish these for supper," she said. "And then we'll be eatin' what I got preserved in the root cellar for the winter." She took a sharp look at us leaning together over the table. "What are you two up to?"

"Nothing," Stephen said. "Just cleaning lanterns."

She kept looking at us till I moved away, still polishing that dish so hard it's a wonder I didn't wear a hole in it.

"Humph," she said, and started unloading her basket.

But I was happy. I could read "Man." M-m-m-m.

9

A FEW DAYS LATER, ON A MONDAY IN OCTOBER, MR. Gorin showed up. This time we had no visitors in the hotel, and it was cold, so we were sitting in the kitchen house with the fire going, Mittie making bread, me mending sheets, and Stephen, Mat, and Nick playing cards. Mr. Miller had already been in and seen them at it and didn't say anything, so I guess he didn't have things for them to do right then.

When Mr. Gorin came in the kitchen house we all stood up and said, "Afternoon, Mr. Gorin." He told us to sit, so we did, and then he said he had something to tell us. I didn't like hearing those words. It was never something wonderful they wanted to let you know. So I was holding my breath when he started talking again.

"Some changes will be happening soon," he said. "For the cave. I've sold it. It's turned out to be more of a commitment than I anticipated, and I don't have the time to devote to it. The new owner is Dr. John Croghan from Louisville."

We sat there nodding our heads like we knew what was going on, but all we really wanted to know was what was going to happen to us. But we couldn't ask. We were supposed to take whatever came. I wondered how free Stephen was feeling then.

Mr. Gorin went on. "He will be the one making decisions from now on, but he's taking the three of you, Mittie, Stephen, and Charlotte, to start with. What happens after that is up to him. He says he still wants to lease Mat and Nick, too, at least until he gets a feeling for the way things work around here. I imagine it will be pretty quiet here during the winter while he gets organized, but I can't really tell you. Well, that's all." And he turned around and left us sitting there.

I was relieved I got to stay on at the cave, but Stephen looked like he'd been hit on the head with a box of rocks. He was having trouble realizing Mr. Gorin had sold him without one second thought. He hadn't said goodbye or even looked back when he left. I guess that showed Stephen how he wasn't so different from the rest of us. I couldn't help feeling sad for him. And I was feeling sad for me, too, wondering if I'd ever get to know how to read and write.

"He sold us?" Stephen finally said.

"Why you so surprised?" Mittie said without even turning round. "We's just part of the cave, like the rocks. You takin' it too personal."

"What about Mama and Tandy? I thought . . . I . . ." He stood up and went out the door real fast.

"He better not be thinkin' he'll talk to Mr. Gorin 'bout this,"

Mittie said. "It's done. No matter what Stephen wants, it's done."

I knew Stephen believed Mr. Gorin liked him and thought he was special. And probably that was right, Mr. Gorin *did* like him, and *did* think he was special—but he still could sell him if he wanted to, or needed to. Mittie had it right—it wasn't personal, it was business.

Later Stephen told me he'd gone after Mr. Gorin and it had turned out just as Mittie had said it would. The deal with Dr. Croghan was done, Stephen was sold along with the cave, Mr. Gorin wished him luck, the end. He did learn that his mama and brother would be staying at Mr. Gorin's in Glasgow, and that Dr. Croghan had said he could have a pass to go see them, which was some good news for him.

A few days after that, Dr. Croghan came to the cave to look things—and us—over. We were peeking out the kitchen house windows trying to get a look at him, too, even when we knew that wouldn't tell us anything about how he was. What we saw was a sturdy-built man, thick in the shoulders, square-headed, mustache so tidy you knew he spent a lot of time fussing with it.

Mr. Miller came and got us and took us up to the hotel porch, where we stood shivering in the cold while he named us off to Dr. Croghan. The only thing Dr. Croghan said was, "Are they good workers?"

Mr. Miller said yes, we were.

"All right," Dr. Croghan said. "Mr. Miller will still be supervising you, but I'll be watching."

And we knew he would be. We already knew he was different

from Mr. Gorin. More serious about his possessions, more particular.

The rest of the day, he was marching around the property asking questions, writing things down, drawing in the dirt with a stick.

Soon after that, wagons started bringing in materials. He was going to spend the cold months getting a better hotel built, and Stephen and Mat and Nick would be helping to do it, so we would all be together for the winter, after all.

Owners always seemed to figure slaves could do anything they were told to do, whether they'd ever done it before or not. So Mat and Nick and Stephen were learning new things about building every day, and Mittie and me, we were kept busy cooking for the workers and cleaning up after them. We were all working our best so's not to give Dr. Croghan a reason to get rid of us.

I'll say this for our new owner—he didn't pinch his pennies. He made sure there was plenty of food for everybody—we weren't spending the winter living off what Mittie had in jars in the cellar at all. We were eating even better than with Mr. Gorin.

Stephen, though, was pretty quiet. He didn't talk about it, but I knew he hadn't got over being sold. He did tell me he worried about seeing his family again, since he was afraid to ask Dr. Croghan about the travel pass. And he was missing his cave because he was spending so much time working on the building.

That was a long winter, and it was cold, too. As soon as I could every night, after the supper mess was all cleaned up, I'd go in my cabin, build up the fire, and just sit there feeling lonely and wondering if there would ever be time for me to learn to read. We were all busy, but somehow we weren't like a group anymore. We were just a bunch of people doing separate things.

Nick must have been feeling some of that as well. One early morning he said, "We need some festivity around here. We've all been working too much and letting the dark and the cold drag us down. Tonight we're going to dance."

Mittie humphed, as usual, and Stephen gave a weak little smile. But Mat, he surprised us all by pulling a harmonica out of his pocket and playing a tune. I never had seen him with that before, and he was good. "Where'd you learn that?" I asked.

"This thing was my daddy's," he said. "'Fore he passed, he gave it to me, taught me a little about how to play it. The rest I just worked on myself. It's been good company to me." And he played some more.

All that day I was waiting for night so we could have our music and our dancing. I was also hoping it would help Stephen feel better. After supper and cleaning up, Mittie made us some popcorn and hot chocolate. We had Dr. Croghan to thank for these luxuries. Then Mat played, and Nick grabbed me around the waist and we set off, jumping around the kitchen house. Around and around the table we went, and we started in laughing like we couldn't stop.

Nick set me down in a chair and grabbed up Mittie. 'Fore she even had time to harrumph, he had her going around with him. I looked at Stephen sitting there, his face blank, and I got up and put my arms out to him.

"I don't know how," he started saying, but I just pulled him up and put his hands on my waist and my hands on his shoulders, and off we went. We were bumping into Mittie and Nick and then going by them, and then bumping again, and we all were laughing. It was the first time I'd heard Mittie laugh. Then Mat was laughing, too, so he couldn't play anymore.

But that was all right. We'd had our dancing and our laughing and our treats, and we were all feeling good—and like a group again.

Around the beginning of March the hotel was done, and while it was being fixed up, Dr. Croghan had gotten new roads built, too, making it easier to get to the cave. One road came right by the front of the hotel, and somehow he got the hotel made into a regular stagecoach stop. Dr. Croghan, we started figuring, had lots more influential friends than Mr. Gorin had. And more money as well.

10

ONCE THE HOTEL WAS FINISHED, WE WERE HAVING A little break before the tourists started coming in. Since we had some extra time, I asked Stephen again about the reading and writing. And he said all right. Trouble was, we didn't have a safe place to do it. We didn't know Dr. Croghan's feelings on the subject, though we knew Mr. Miller wouldn't like it. And there were still some workmen around who might also take exception to Stephen and me reading.

Stephen said, "We could go in the cave. It'd be safe in there."

"Oh, no," I said. "I'm not going in there."

"You know, Mittie always says that cave's a serious place meant for serious things—not just having folks come look at it. Don't you think learning to read is a serious thing?"

When he put it like that, how was I going to say no? Didn't I want to learn? Wasn't I serious about that? Oh, he was smart. He had me. "But I'm scared of that place. Nothing but dark, and only one way out."

"There's more to it than dark," he told me. "And as long as you got one way out, you can always leave, right?"

He kept backing me into a corner, making it hard for me to disagree. I was hoping he was as good a teacher as he was an arguer, 'cause I sure wasn't keeping up with him there.

"Just let me show you," he said. "We don't have to go very far in to be private. We'll bring lots of lanterns. You'll see."

How could I say no? So I had to say, "I'll try it. *Once.* If I don't like it, we'll have to think of something else."

"Fine. That's fine. Tonight, then. After supper."

So even though I tried to slow that day down, suppertime came, and went, and then it was time. Mittie went off to her quarters, and Nick and Mat had finally given up playing horseshoes in the last of the daylight. And then there I was, standing at the mouth of the cave, holding the lantern Stephen had brought from the storage shed for me, my knees knocking together in fear.

"You want to take my arm?" Stephen asked. He was carrying his own two lanterns, one lit, the other, like mine, unlit. "We can go in with just one lamp, and light the others when we get where we're going."

I nodded and grabbed hold of his arm. I could feel his solid muscle, and somehow, knowing he was strong under his coat made me feel better. It didn't make good sense, I knew that, but I still felt better.

It was just big, that cave, that's all I could say about it as we started in. I was looking for what the visitors thought was so special, but I didn't see it unless it was only the bigness. The ceiling must have been way up high, 'cause I couldn't see it, and the sides, I couldn't even tell how far away they were in the dark. And the path went straight on into more dark. More big, big dark. I couldn't credit that all this was made by drips of water, no matter what Stephen or anybody else said.

And it was chilly in there, not hot like I thought. Stephen laughed when I asked him how close we were to hell. He said it must be located somewhere else, not in Kentucky.

As long as I could still see the opening behind me I did all right, even while it was getting dark outside, too. But as soon as we turned around a corner and were all the way *inside*, I started breathing real fast. Stephen's lamp made such a small light against so much dark. I was hanging on to him hard.

"We're going to stop here a minute," he said. "To let you get used to being in here. To let you see there's nothing to be worrying about."

So we stood there, me still grabbing his arm, and we waited. It was quiet. Extra quiet. Almost like you could feel the quiet, like it felt heavy against you.

"Quiet," I said.

Stephen just smiled at me and nodded.

"Dark, too," I said.

He lifted up his lantern. "We've got light. When I first came here, this fellow who taught me how to guide, first thing he told me was to protect my light. What he said was, light's what'll save you, body and soul. We've got lots of it. And I know how to light a lantern in the dark if it blows out. I practiced over and over till I could do it. As long as you're with me, you've got nothing to worry about."

He made me believe him. Anybody who could light a lantern in the dark, underground, was somebody I could be safe with.

While we stood there I asked him something I'd been wondering about. "Who did teach you guiding? What made Mr. Gorin think you'd be so good at it?"

"There wasn't any plan. He just didn't have much choice. He only owned me and Mama and Tandy. And I think I told you Tandy isn't the hardest worker. So when Mr. Gorin bought the cave, I was all he had to come here. The son of the previous owner, a white boy, he'd been guiding for a long time and he was ready for something else. So ready, he didn't care he was passing his job on to a slave. He'd have passed it to anybody just so he could get out of there. He spent four days showing me around, and then he was gone. But by then I'd already gotten kind of bewitched by the place. It was all nothing but a surprise. A lucky surprise."

My breaths were coming more normal by then, so Stephen started walking, pulling me along, since I wasn't going to turn loose of him. He walked slow, but it still seemed too fast for me.

We made some more turns and then I had to give up trying to remember how I could get out. I had to put all my trust in Stephen, which wasn't hard to do. He kept talking, telling me about the things we were passing, how this rock was called Giant's

Coffin (not a name I liked hearing, I have to say), and this place was called Gothic Avenue, and all like that, but I could hardly listen, I was so scared. And no matter how fancy the places were named, they looked like nothing but rocks to me.

Finally we stopped. "How long have we been in here?" I said. It felt like hours.

"About twenty minutes," he told me.

I had to laugh. "Are you joking with me? It's got to be longer than that."

"Nope. You'll see on the way out."

"Is this the place?" We were in a kind of small rock room. After all the big spaces we'd passed through, it seemed almost cozy.

"Yep. This is it. We got us some formations here we can sit on, so we should be nice and comfy."

He lit the other two lanterns. With three of them making light, I could see our room was about the size of my cabin. The lamps made it real bright, and warm, too. I sat down on a rock, glad to be sitting and not standing on my wobbly legs.

Stephen took a newspaper out of his pocket, and a stub of a pencil. "The first thing we're doing is learning how to write 'Charlotte.'" He made some marks on the edge of the paper. "That spells 'Charlotte,'" he told me.

I studied it. The word seemed nice. Long and elegant. I liked it. "That's my name," I said, and felt shy saying it. "Spell 'Stephen' now."

He made more marks.

"We've got some things the same," I said, pointing.

"Those are called 'E,' and those are called 'H,' and those are called 'T,' " he told me. Then he wrote out what he said was the alphabet, and told me all the names. I recognized "E" and "H" and "T" now, but no way could I ever remember all the others. He told me how each one sounded—more things I couldn't remember. He showed me in the newspaper where there were "E's" and "H's" and "T's." It turned out they could be big and little, and sometimes big ones and little ones didn't even look the same. I was starting to wonder if I really did want to learn all that. Maybe Mittie had it right—what was I ever going to have to read? Maybe I just wanted to be able to write my name.

I told Stephen this, and he said, "We can start with that." He wanted me to copy out what he wrote for my name, but I didn't know even how to hold on to the pencil. He put his hand over mine and showed me how, and helped me write out my name on the edge of the newspaper. It didn't look exactly like the one he'd written, but almost. Then he made me do it over and over. And then I was doing it all by myself. I could write my name!

"I think that's enough for our first lesson," Stephen told me, and he put a corner of the newspaper we'd been writing on in the flame of the lamp and burned it all up.

"What are you doing?" I asked him. "I want that! I want to look at my name and practice making it."

"And what if somebody sees you doing that? Or finds that piece of paper? There'd be a lot of trouble, and not only for you.

I'd be having some, too. If we're going to keep doing this, you've got to learn to keep it secret. Even from Mittie and Nick and Mat. We don't want to be doing anything that'll get them in trouble."

"But how am I going to remember about writing my name?"

He took my finger and wrote with it in the dirt on the floor. "See? There's CHARLOTTE in the dirt." He rubbed it out with his shoe. Then he stood me up and walked me to the wall and wrote CHARLOTTE on the wall with his finger and then with mine. Course, we couldn't see it, but I knew it was there. "You can practice that way. It's safer like that."

He was right about getting out of the cave. It did feel faster. Maybe 'cause I was thinking so much about how I could now write CHARLOTTE.

11

THE NEXT NIGHT I WOKE UP. I DIDN'T KNOW THE TIME, but it was dark dark, no sign of sunrise, and my stomach was growling. I reckoned I didn't eat enough supper. Or maybe I was still too excited about writing my name to even think about eating. In fact, my finger was sore on the end from all the times I'd written CHARLOTTE on the wall in my cabin.

Everywhere else I'd been I'd have just had to stay hungry, but this place was different. I started thinking about the piece of Mittie's chess pie left from supper, and I decided that's what I wanted. So I got up, lit my lamp, put on my shoes and my shawl over my nightdress, and started to the kitchen house.

It was real quiet out, and nippy in the air, and not a light anywhere except a tiny bit of starlight to break the dark. As I got closer to the kitchen house, it seemed to me I could see the windows a little even in the dark. Had Mittie gone off to bed leaving a lantern burning? That wasn't like her.

I pushed on the door, but it was stuck and wouldn't open up. So I pushed more till I heard this whisper from the other side saying, "Who's there?" I couldn't tell who was saying that.

"Me. Charlotte. That you, Mittie?"

I heard some more whispering, and then the door getting unbolted, and there was Mittie saying, "Get in here quick."

I squeezed in, and while she was closing the door, I looked around and about jumped out of my skin when I saw there was a man at the kitchen table. A black man looking kind of wild and ragged, and halfway out of his chair like he was ready to run.

I pulled my shawl tight around me and held my breath. "I was just wanting a piece of that chess pie," I said, real soft. "I woke up hungry."

The man sank back into his chair.

Mittie, all dressed, apron and everything, took my arm in her hand so hard I about yelped, and she said, "Charlotte, this here's Denmark. Denmark, show her your back."

Denmark got up, turned round, and raised up his tattered shirt. Even by the light of the single candle on the table I could see what he was showing me. I'd seen things like that before—those silvery stripes of old scars, and the red half-healed ones, and the fresh open new ones. Somebody'd been taking the whip to Denmark. A lot.

"Denmark's running?" I said.

"That's right," Mittie said. "I can't do much but feed him, and give him a jacket a visitor left behind, and some food to take to the next stop. Wish we had a place we could put him up for a couple days to rest, but we don't. I got to work on that."

I didn't know why she was telling me unless I'd just come along at the right minute. But I was glad she was. I said, "Anything I can do?"

"Mostly keep quiet about this," Mittie said. "Can you do that?"

"Sure. Easy. Where's he going now?"

"We're a hundred and some miles from Ohio, and that's a free state. He only has to get across the river and he's free, even if he's not all the way safe."

"How far's Canada?" I asked.

"A lot more. But there's help across the river, if that's where he wants to go."

"Over a hundred miles. That's a long way."

"He's come farther than that already. He can do more."

All this time Denmark didn't say a word. He just looked plumb done in. Seemed a crime to be sending him out again in the cold and the dark without rest. But Mittie was right—we had no place to safely hide him.

"You know how he should go?" I asked Mittie.

"Course I know. I been here a long time, girl," she said to me. "I know a lot more than I tell. And I know who's gonna help him at his next stop, too."

"You've done this before," I said.

"More than once. Now you take your pie and go."

I forgot all about being hungry. "Only if you're sure I can't do something to help."

"Get on to bed," she said.

So I took my pie, and carried it back to my place, and ate it down, hardly tasting it. There were runners coming through here! With all these people around, a lot of the time! Were those runners stupid? Or just desperate? Course, I knew the answer to that. And maybe really they were smart. Maybe the best place to not get noticed was in a bunch of other people.

I was through sleeping for that night, that was for sure.

The next day I kept waiting for a chance to talk to Mittie, but we were busy and there were a lot of Dr. Croghan's workers coming in and going out all the time. Finally, when we were out bringing up water from the well, I whispered to her, "How long have you been doing this? How many have you helped?"

"I'm not sayin' one word 'less you cross your heart, and cross your eyes, and spit, and promise never to tell anybody what I'm tellin' you."

I did what she said, and I meant it.

"Been doin' it almost since I got here. This place, it's right on the route between way south and free Ohio. Indiana too, but there's not so much help right on the other side of the river there. Makes sense they come by this way. I don't know how many, just there's been some every year I been here. More some years, less others. Mostly in spring and summer, when it's not too cold to sleep out if you got to, and there's food in the fields for the pickin'.

Now hush up about it. Hard to keep a secret, once more than one knows it."

"So why did you tell me?"

She took a deep breath and let it out slow. "I'm old, that's why. There's got to be somebody to keep doing it if I—" She stopped, concentrating on the water buckets. "I think you can. Am I right?"

"I wasn't offering to help just with Denmark last night. I know why they need to run."

We started toward the kitchen house, carrying our buckets, not talking. But I was looking at Mittie in a new way. Who'd have thought?

12

WELL, THE SEASON STARTED AND THE TOURISTS CAME.
They came, and they came, and they all still wanted Stephen.
Nick's nose was bent out of shape about that, but once the visitors
took his tours, they liked him, too. Just he wasn't known as the big
explorer Stephen was.

One day I was sitting in the kitchen house—always felt good to
get off my feet for a bit—polishing silver teaspoons, when Nick
came in carrying a jar with what looked like water in it.

"If you're going to bring in water," I told him, "we need a lot
more than that."

He put the jar down on the table and said, "Take a better
look."

So I did, and I saw there was a fish in that jar. A little white
fish.

"Now I'm glad we won't be drinking from that," I said. "I like
my drinks without the swimmy things in them."

"Look harder at that swimmy thing."

I was asking myself, How much can you look at a fish? but I did what he said, and I gave it a good hard stare, and then I saw what he meant. That fish had no eyes! It had these bumps where eyes should have been, but there were no eyes there. I looked up at him, and he was laughing.

"Where did you get that fish?" I asked. "What's wrong with it?"

"Nothin's wrong. They're all like that. All the fish in that river Stephen found."

"There's *fish* under there, too?" That place was seeming stranger and stranger. "Why don't they have eyes?"

He laughed again, the way he did at so many things I said. "What have they got to look at? It's dark as the inside of a bear in there. Makes 'em easy to catch, when they can't see you comin'."

"What are you going to do with it?"

"Thought I'd show it to Dr. Croghan. Maybe he'll want to sell 'em to the tourists. They're kind of small for it, but he could even sell 'em stuffed."

Turned out Dr. Croghan jumped on the idea of selling the fish, alive *and* stuffed—and so did the visitors. So Nick, he was getting to feel big, telling everybody on his tours he was the one that found the blind white fish in the river. I wasn't going to be the one to tell him he wouldn't have been finding fish if Stephen hadn't found the river first.

I kept looking for another time Stephen and I could work on my reading again, even if it meant going back in that cave, but it was hard. When Stephen did have a minute to himself, he was plain dog-tired. And there were always too many people around to explain why the two of us had to go off together somewhere private.

We finally got a minute to talk, and made a plan. We decided on after supper, once Mittie went off to her cabin, and after Nick and Mat finished with their horseshoes. We'd go in the cave just for a little while, to work on my alphabet sounds. I knew Stephen was wanting to go to sleep more than he wanted to be doing lessons with me, so I was thankful.

Course Mat and Nick stuck with those horseshoes till I thought they'd be at it all night. But finally it got too dark to see what they were doing, and they gave up, and turned in, and Stephen and I came creeping out of our cabins. I've got to say, going back in that cave wasn't something I was crazy about. I had to remind myself we'd have plenty of lanterns, and Stephen's strong arm, and the alphabet that was going to help me read words.

First, we had to get lanterns from the shed next the kitchen house, so we started up the hill to do that. Then Stephen stopped, and he held out his hand to make me stop. Before I could ask what was going on, he put his finger to his lips so I wouldn't. We stood there in the dark, real still. I knew he was listening, but I didn't know what for. All I could tell was that it was real, real quiet.

And then I knew that's what he was listening to: the quiet. 'Cause there should have been crickets. They were usually singing their heads off till you wanted to come out and gag each one of them. Something was scaring them, making them be quiet. And it couldn't have been us because they were quiet even before we came along.

First I thought of a skunk there in the bushes, and I really didn't want to run into one of those. I'd done that once, and once is enough, I can tell you that. Then I was feeling cross. Seemed like everything in the world was trying to get in the way of me learning to read, once I'd finally got up the gumption to start.

I must have made some kind of sound, thinking about that, 'cause Stephen put his hand on my arm and gave it a squeeze, like "hush up." Then we heard a twig snap. That's when I knew what was in there. When animals move in bushes, they make a rustly kind of scurrying noise. When a person moves in the bushes, they try to be quiet—just now and then making a little sound, like when they step on a twig. If those crickets had been singing, we wouldn't have heard it at all.

I looked up at Stephen. I could hardly see him in the dark, but from the grip he had on my arm, I could tell how still he was standing.

Then this whisper came out from the bushes, this voice saying, "Please."

"Who's in there?" I said, and I bent down to where I'd heard the voice. Stephen had to let loose my arm.

"Help me," said the voice.

I should have been scared to death, and I was, but I knew what was happening, and I'd said I'd help. What else could I do?

"Come on out," I said. "You can't stay in there if we're going to help."

So this person crawled from under the bushes. It was so dark we could hardly tell, but it seemed like a girl. A young one. And if anybody saw us with her, it'd be the worst kind of trouble for all of us.

"Come on," I said, putting my arm around her. "Let's get up to the kitchen house. Quick, now." And I started on the path with her. I could feel her heart beating next to me. My own was going about as fast. I took a few steps before I realized Stephen wasn't coming, too. I whispered back to him. "Come on!"

"I . . . I don't know," he said.

"I can't wait out here," I told him. "Come or not, but I've got to go." And I kept moving with the runner. I saw the hotel windows were all dark, so that was good. But you still never knew who could be looking.

Inside, first thing, I lit a lantern but closed the shields so the light was low. I could see my runner was young—about fourteen or so, only a few years younger than me, but she seemed like a child. Thin, and dirty, too, and shivering hard. I took a couple of the towels Mittie used to cover her bread while it was rising, and I threw them over her shoulders. Then I sat her down and took the kettle from the hob where it stayed warm all night, and started making her some tea.

When I put the cup down in front of her, she looked up at me, and she had big tears in her eyes.

"Go on, drink it," I told her, "while I get you something to eat. Looks like you been walking for a long time."

I kept prattling along like that while I fixed her a plate, the way Mittie would have, and all the while I was feeling my heart hammering hard and scared. And I was wondering what had happened to Stephen. Was he still standing out there in the dark, or had he gone back to his cabin, or what?

When I was putting down that plate, there came a knock at the door. My heart banged in my chest, and I whispered, "Who's there?"

Stephen whispered back, "It's me."

I unbolted the door and opened it. Stephen squeezed himself in, shut the door, bolted it again, and put a chair up against it, too. He wasn't taking any chances—except the big one of coming in to start with. Then he just stood there looking all stiff and saucer-eyed, the way I must have looked when I went inside the cave. The way I should have been looking right then if I'd had good sense, except I was so busy seeing to this girl.

"That's just Stephen," I said to her. "Nothing to worry about with either one of us."

She kept eating, the way you do when you've been hungry for a long time and you're not sure when you'll get to eat again.

"What's your name?" I asked her. "You know Stephen. I'm Charlotte. What can we call you?"

In this little tired voice, she said, "Delphine."

"Why, that's a pretty name," I told her, and I meant it. "Where you coming from, Delphine?"

"Alabama." She swallowed. "I didn't know it was so far to get free. And that it would be cold some nights, even in summer. They chased after me a long time, but I kept running and hiding. I don't know when they gave up, or even if they did."

"When did you set out?"

She shook her head. "I don't know. Some days ago." And she shivered again. I was starting to figure she wasn't only tired and hungry—she was sick.

I turned to Stephen and said, "I've got to go get Mittie. I don't know what to do next here."

"What about her?" He pointed to Delphine.

"What about her? You stay here with her while I get Mittie."

"But what if—"

"What if nothing," I said, cutting him off. "You've got to." Hard to believe this was the same Stephen who went across Bottomless Pit, and into other places in the cave everybody else was scared to go.

I went to get Mittie and she came awake in a second, almost like she'd been waiting for me. She said it was because she was an old lady and she didn't sleep so well anymore.

"Stephen's there with her?" she asked me, sounding kind of surprised.

"Something wrong with that?" I asked her. I had my back turned to her while she got dressed.

"Not wrong," she said. "Just didn't think he'd be one liked to do this kind of helpin'."

"I'm pretty sure he doesn't like it," I said, "but he was there when we found her, so now he's in it."

"The two of you was out walkin' in the dark?" Mittie said.

"It's not like that," I told her. "He's teaching me to read. We've been having trouble finding time, and a place to do it."

"You're learnin' to read?" Mittie said, her hand on the door latch. She was whispering, but somehow it seemed like she was screaming. "We ain't got enough to worry about round here without you doin' that? You know how hard it is to keep *one* secret? I kept mine for this long 'cause there wasn't nobody else to tell. But now you know, and you got your own secret to keep, too. That just *begs* for trouble."

"Mittie, we've got Delphine to worry about tonight. We can figure out the rest later, all right?"

By the time we got to the kitchen house, I don't think Stephen would have been any happier to see the angel Gabriel than he was to see us. Delphine had finished eating and drinking her tea, and she'd put her head right down on the table and gone to sleep.

Mittie touched her on the forehead and she didn't wake up at all, but Mittie said, "She burnin' up. No way in the world this girl is going to travel on tonight. We got to get her to a safe place where she can rest and get better."

"We have empty slave cabins," Stephen said. "We can put her in one of those."

"And take a chance on Mr. Miller or some fool tourist walking in on her?" She gave him one of her hard stares. "You crazy? We need a place nobody'll go."

"But we don't have . . ." he began, and then stopped. He understood before I did what she meant. "No."

"You know how I'm always sayin' that's a serious place for serious things? What do you think this is?" When he didn't answer, she went on. "This child needs to sleep. That's nature's medicine, and that's what she needs. In a safe place. A place only one person would know about. And that person is you. Up till you there's been white men guidin'. I wanted to use that cave for my runners, but I couldn't. Now I can. 'Cause of you."

I had to admire her. In only a few words, she'd touched Stephen's compassion and his pride. She'd let him know he wasn't the kind of person to cause suffering to a sick, desperate child, and that he alone would be clever enough to find a secret place where she could be safe. I didn't see how he could keep saying no.

"She could go in that little room where you taught me to write," I said. "Is it in the way of any of the tours?"

He shook his head unhappily.

"You *writin'*, too?" Mittie said, just about hopping.

I almost had to laugh. "We can leave her with lots of lanterns and blankets and food, and tell her we'll be coming in to check on her. It won't be for more than a day or two. There's no choice—we have no other place to keep her and she can't move on."

Stephen looked like something was hurting him, but he knew he was beat. He blew out a big noisy breath and said, "Oh, all right."

So before I knew it, I was back in the cave with Stephen and Delphine. Mittie, for all her talk about caves and serious purposes, wouldn't put her foot in there. I kept saying I didn't want to, either, but somehow there I was again, never mind how dizzy with fear I was.

We fixed Delphine up in our little classroom with a bunch of lanterns and oil, food and blankets. Me, I'd have been jumping out of my skin at the idea of being in there all alone, but she didn't seem bothered. Maybe she was just too sick to care.

Stephen told her over and over how she shouldn't even think about trying to leave, she should stay put in there till he came back. She kept nodding her head yes. I could tell all she wanted to do was put it down again and shut her eyes. So finally she did that, and she was sleeping before we could get ourselves ready to leave.

Stephen wasn't happy, no doubt about it, even if he didn't say anything. It showed by the way he was walking out of the cave, all stiff-legged, and stiff-backed, and stiff-necked. I kept quiet. Nothing I could say was going to change anything, in spite of the fact that I wanted to ask him what he'd have done if he'd been alone on that path when Delphine spoke out.

If I thought he'd have walked on by, I'd never have wanted to talk to him ever again. But I didn't think that's what he'd have done. And I didn't want to hear him tell me something different.

13

DELPHINE STAYED IN THE CAVE FOR TWO DAYS BEFORE she was ready to go. During the day Stephen checked on her in between tours, and he took me there to see to her at night. As long as she stayed sick, she was just fine with being in the cave. But as soon as she was feeling better, she wanted out.

Stephen was real nice with her, telling her there wasn't a thing to worry about, that she was safe, and that she needed to get better so she would be strong enough to go the rest of the way. But he wasn't talking so nice to me. He was hardly talking to me at all. As if he blamed me for there being a runner in our bushes. I wanted to talk to him about that, but I could wait. We had to get Delphine on her way first.

Mittie, she kept worrying Mr. Miller or somebody would notice what was going on, now that there was more than just her in it and we had a runner in the cave. I worried, too. But I kept reminding myself that folks only saw what they were looking for. And mostly what they were interested in was their own doings. As long as you weren't getting in the way of what they wanted, they mostly weren't paying any attention to you. Anyway, the tourists didn't know how the routines worked around the place, so they wouldn't know if something wasn't right. And as long as everything was working smooth, Mr. Miller wasn't paying much attention either. Still, we needed to be careful, and we were. We were just nervous all the time, that's all.

It didn't take long for Nick to figure something was up. Even at breakfast the morning after we found Delphine, his nose was twitching. Especially when Stephen told him to avoid a certain section of the cave if he decided to do any exploring the next few days. By suppertime he'd had more time to think, and he was suspecting.

"Is it my imagination, or is everybody but me and Mat bein' jumpy, and not so talkative as usual?"

"Must be your imagination," Stephen said, sort of sharp.

"Oh, now I know somethin's goin' on," Nick said. "When Stephen starts talkin' like that. Who you mad at, Stephen? I thought you were the kind never got mad at anybody."

"Show's how much you know," Stephen said.

Mittie and I threw a glance at each other, and I saw the same look going between Nick and Mat.

Mittie peered out the kitchen-house window to make sure nobody was coming, and she said, "What would you say if I told you we was helpin' a runner?"

My mouth kind of came open all by itself. What happened to

this big secret Mittie was so set on keeping? Now she was telling Mat and Nick, who didn't need to know anything about it. Or maybe she figured they did, since they were going to be in the cave where they might come across our runner by accident. Or maybe she just figured, what was the difference, everybody else knew now, why not Mat and Nick, too? I knew she wasn't going to tell me why, so I just shut my mouth and kept it that way.

Nick and Mat gave each other another kind of look then, and Nick said, "Now I get why you're telling us where not to do any explorin'. And we'll do that whenever you say to. But don't tell us one more word. We're playin' like we never heard you say that, and if you did say it, we ain't believin' it, and if we're believin' it, we don't want nothin' to do with it. Any trouble you want to cook up around here, you're welcome to keep it all to yourselves."

"All right, then," Mittie said. "I never told you nothin', and if you think you heard me say somethin', well, you're wrong. Now cross your hearts, and cross your eyes, and spit, and swear you never heard a thing."

"Fine," Nick said, and so did Mat. "Now, Mat, will you please pass me them sweet potatoes?"

The next night, when it was real dark and late, Stephen and I went in the cave to fetch Delphine. I wondered if I'd ever get used to feeling so scared about going in there. Or about what we were doing.

"I tell you," Delphine said to us, "I'll be real glad to get out of here."

I understood what she was saying, but Stephen, he didn't.

"Don't you feel safe in here?" he asked her. "If I'd been hiding in here, I would."

"Then what about the . . . the *things* in here?" she asked.

"What things are you talking about? The cave crickets? They're harmless."

"I ain't talkin' about no crickets. Not 'less they're wearin' shoes. What I heard was somebody walkin'."

"Oh," Stephen said. "That probably *was* somebody walking. We've got people in here every day, taking tours. Sounds echo and travel."

"Not *people*," Delphine said. "Just one or two."

"Could have been water dripping."

"I know what water drippin' sounds like," Delphine said, and she was getting piqued. "And it wasn't that. 'Sides, I saw somethin'. Somethin' movin' in here. Just on the edge of the light. Somethin' shaped like a person."

I got cold all over then, and took some quick looks around, but I didn't see anything, thank the Lord. "A person?" I asked her.

"Not a person," Stephen said, real definite. "Couldn't be. Without a lantern nobody can find their way around in here. Besides, nobody comes in here alone except the guides. It's way too easy to get lost."

"I know what I saw," Delphine said. Her bottom lip was sticking out in a stubborn way, and I could see where her gumption to run came from.

"I think we don't have time to be arguing about that," I said. "We got to get you on your way."

We stopped at the mouth of the cave, looking out into the cool, moonless night. Mittie waited in the trees, holding a flour sack with fried chicken in it, and biscuits, apples, and carrots, and a couple of baked potatoes. We hurried to join her, and she handed the bag over to Delphine, saying, "It's kind of heavy."

Delphine grabbed it up and hugged it to her skinny chest. "I don't mind," she said. "Not one bit."

Mittie sat herself down on a stump, so slow you could barely see her moving, and, by the shielded light of Stephen's lamp, drew a map in the dirt with a stick, showing Delphine how to go. All that time I was looking around and around me, whether for spirits from the cave, or Mr. Miller, or some restless visitor, I wasn't even sure, and my heart was beating so hard I had trouble catching my breath.

Stephen helped Mittie stand up, and as soon as she did, she gave Delphine a quick, hard hug. First time I ever saw Mittie touch anybody, except for that one time she patted my knee. Then Stephen shook Delphine by the hand and said, "Godspeed," and I stepped up to hug her, too. Holding that scrawny girl in my arms, I got a rush of tears to my eyes. She was so young, and had such a long hard way yet to go. All that courage and hope made it hard for me to breathe.

She went off down the path—a little shadow fading away from us.

As soon as she was gone, Mittie hustled herself off to bed, but I stood on the side of that path with Stephen, looking at the way Delphine had gone off, even long after I couldn't see her anymore.

Stephen stayed there with me. Watching her go, I wondered why I didn't go on with her. It would have been so easy. I told myself the time wasn't right, or I wasn't ready, or I wanted to go alone. But I knew that was all wrong. I was scared—that was the truth—and I was standing next to a big reason why I didn't want to go. I didn't want to go away from Stephen.

14

STEPHEN AND I WALKED TOGETHER UP THE PATH TOWARD our cabins, not talking. But I could feel him next to me being all hard-mouthed and stiff-backed.

"You might as well get it off your chest," I told him.

"My chest is pretty full tonight," he told me, like he was giving me a warning.

So we stepped off the path and sat down on a log there in the dark.

"Now, before you start in," I said, "I know you weren't happy about having Delphine in your cave. About having Delphine here at all. But what do you think we should have done when she said 'Please' to us from inside that bush?"

He put his elbows on his knees and hung his head down, shaking it. "If I had my way, she wouldn't have come here ever."

I couldn't help it. I put my hand on his knee, kind of comforting him, and I said, "But she did. You think we had a choice? What else could we have done?"

"Nothing. I know that. We had to help her. But the way I was feeling the whole time she was hiding in there—I don't ever want to be feeling like that again, or for that long. I wasn't sleeping at all. And I was jumping at every sound, thinking we were about to get caught. Don't tell me you weren't scared."

"Oh, I was scared. And I wasn't sleeping, neither."

"You talked about running. You could have gone with her."

"I could," I said.

"Why didn't you?"

I was quiet, thinking. Then I said, "I guess I'm scared of that, too. But someday I want to know what free feels like. Why don't *you* go?"

He didn't need to think. His answer came right out. "The cave. Something's between me and that cave. I know now I could get sold away from here, so it's more important than ever that I do as much exploring as I can while I'm still here. I need that."

The way he was talking, it was almost like he was praying. I knew he liked exploring in there, but till then I didn't know how deep his feeling about that big hole in the ground went. He loved it.

"They're brave to go, aren't they?" I said, to keep him talking. "And they've got to be leaving something bad to go through all this. Don't they?"

"I believe that. I just wish they weren't coming through here."

"Well, they are. We can help, or not. Nick and Mat, they won't. I understand that, but they're wrong. I think about if I was the one running. Wouldn't I be wanting somebody brave enough to help me?"

That made him quiet for a while. Then he breathed real deep again and stood up. "Not everybody can be that brave."

He stood there with his back to me, and he said, "Maybe I *should* run. Away from worrying about runners, and getting caught, and what would come after that."

"You've just been telling me why you can't," I said. "What you have now is the worry you know. Running, that's a worry you don't know."

I was surprising myself. I should have been convincing him *to* run. But it felt wrong. That's all I can say. It just felt wrong for me to be pushing him to leave something he loved so much, and that he wouldn't be able to find anywhere else. What I wanted was for him to feel that way about me.

When he talked, I could hear a kind of smile in his voice. "I don't know why you think you need to learn reading and writing. You've already got more sense than lots of people with all kinds of schooling and learning."

I liked that. So I said, "You're reminding me now. When are we going to get back to our lessons? I can write 'Charlotte' in my sleep. In fact, a lot of times, I do. Now I'm ready to be learning some more."

"You are the hardest person to say no to," he said. "All right.

How about tomorrow after the others go to bed? Provided we don't have any more rescuing to do." And he walked off, leaving me there, not even saying good night, like he'd just had all he could take of me.

I sat a while longer, weary inside and out. How did those folks decide to run? How did they do it, just go, not knowing what was ahead of them, nor how to get anywhere, nor who would help? How miserable did you have to be to do that? A lot more miserable than me, for sure, since right then I felt like I couldn't get up and run even if I knew there was a pack of dogs after me right round the corner.

I finally went off to bed, wondering where Delphine would be sleeping the next day, and the next, and however many days it would take her to get where she was going, if she even knew where that was.

The night after Delphine left, Stephen and I were in the cave with a newspaper for my lesson. He was all business with me for a hard hour. By the end of it I was reading some lines in the paper— but maybe it was only 'cause I'd said them so many times after Stephen that I thought I was.

I wrote my name on the edge of the paper to show him I hadn't forgotten how, and then watched him burn it. He took me to the mouth of the cave, not talking the whole way, and told me good night before we came out. He didn't make any new plan for another lesson, either. I watched him go up the path like something was chasing him.

I knew why. It was because of me that he'd had to help Delphine, and now he felt like he'd be forced into helping any runners that came our way, even if he didn't want to. I'd messed up the comfortable arrangement he had for himself and he wasn't happy about it—or about me.

I really did understand all that. But I still wanted to cry.

15

WE STAYED SO BUSY WE WERE BARELY SLEEPING. DR. Croghan was a good businessman, I could see that. People kept pouring in. He advertised, and got newspaper articles printed, and he was starting to make a little book for the visitors telling about the cave, the history of it, and new things happening there, like Stephen's discoveries.

He'd kept a tight eye on us, too, the way he'd said he would, till he got to know how we worked. All winter he was around a lot, watching and correcting and managing. Then he laid back some, I guess after seeing how we could work without so much interfering. Come summer, he seemed satisfied to leave us completely to Mr. Miller for overseeing.

Once again, between his tours and his exploring, Stephen was spending more time in that cave than out of it. I didn't know how much of that was trying to stay away from me, and how much was to keep from getting mixed up with any more runners.

Nick was around more than Stephen, and I've got to say, he was easier than Stephen. Maybe he wasn't the most serious person in the world, but I already had plenty of serious going on. Sometimes it just felt good to be in the company of a happy person.

One day Nick found me where I was hanging out sheets in back of the hotel. He popped up from behind a sheet, half scaring me to death, and he had a bunch of wildflowers in his hand.

I was standing there patting my chest 'cause my heart was beating so fast from being scared, and he was bowing in front of me, and handing me the flowers. I took them before I thought. *Then* I thought. What did this mean, him giving me flowers?

"They're pretty," I said.

"Like you," he said.

I cleared my throat and said, "How come you're not guiding? I thought we had us a full house?"

"They all want Stephen. So he's takin' a big group, and Mat's takin' the ones that are left. Mr. Miller, he says I'm not needed, so . . . Anyway, you get old Nick, the one nobody wants, to come visit with you."

I could see he was feeling sorry for himself and wanted some bucking up. I knew what Mittie'd do if he brought that mopey old face to her. She'd give him some chore and get him out of the way as soon as she could. I felt like doing that, too, but I looked at that face and I couldn't help feeling sorry for him.

"Take hold of that end of the bedsheet," I told him. "The sooner I get these things up on the line, the sooner I can get to some other stuff."

I saw him looking around to tell if anybody could see him hanging laundry. That was about all he'd need to finish him off for that day: hanging laundry instead of guiding. But he took the sheet, sort of hiding behind it, and he helped me hang the rest of the wash. It went fast with two.

Then I had to get to the rest of my chores, but first I put the flowers in water in the kitchen house. After that, he followed me around like a puppy dog, hauling water and wood, and cheering up while he did it. And telling me stories.

". . . So I told that mean old man, 'Thank you, sir, I'll sure remember what you're tellin' me.' Just didn't tell him exactly *how* I'd be rememberin' it." He laughed, and so did I. My mama used to say, "A merry heart makes light the work." She said she thought it came from the Bible, somebody'd told her that. Wherever it came from, it's the truth, that's for sure, and Nick was showing it to me that day.

By suppertime, the two of us were in a kind of a party humor from sharing chores and each other's company all afternoon. Mittie, Stephen, and Mat had their same old glum faces, but Nick and I were feeling good. And somehow that made those others even more low. Funny how that works. Seems there's some folks just can't stand seeing anybody else having a good time. And instead of entering into the good time themselves, they want to sink down even more into their own moping.

Stephen glared at Nick across the table like he was trying to hurt him with just his eyes. I was plenty glad I had the serving to do, so I wasn't in there with them. Once I was done serving, and ready to start the cleaning up, Stephen had gone off somewhere—maybe back inside that precious cave of his—and Mat was off practicing throwing horseshoes. But Nick was still there, helping Mittie out.

"Well, you're just in a generous spirit today," I told him.

"What's wrong with Stephen?" Nick asked me. "Wouldn't you think he'd be happy, what with everybody wantin' him to be their guide? Instead he's actin' like he's got a bug up his backside. You think it's got anything to do with me tellin' him those flowers on the table are the ones I gave you?"

I saw Nick was feeling like himself again—enough to start up something with Stephen. Something that'd make him feel bigger than Stephen, more important. But I wasn't so sure I wanted to be what was in the middle of all that.

"It's just flowers," I said to Nick. "Just flowers. Doesn't mean a thing."

"Means somethin' to me," he said, putting away the last of the dishes.

Without turning around from her work, Mittie said, "Those flowers'd be better off back where you got 'em. Sittin' in that glass, they're gonna do nothin' but cause trouble, no matter what Charlotte thinks."

I said again, "It's just flowers," but I didn't believe it then.

Nick winked at me, and went off to the horseshoes with Mat.

On my way down to my cabin, who was waiting there in the dusk but Stephen. He stepped out from the shadows and said, "Charlotte."

For the second time that day, I was patting my racing heart. Seems that was my day for being taken by surprise.

"Oh, you gave me a fright," I said. "I thought you'd gone back in your cave."

"I wanted to go with you." He made his voice real soft. "I thought we could have another lesson."

How could I say no to another reading and writing lesson?

So I went with him inside that dark cave. I didn't think I'd ever be able to say I was getting used to being in there, but somehow I was. At least, I was getting used to that part from the entrance to the place where I'd been before. And where Delphine had been, too.

Stephen wasn't talking to me while we walked, and I was just as glad. I didn't have much to say myself. But if we had been talking, I think those flowers were something we'd be talking about.

In our little lesson room, Stephen was all business again. He'd said he didn't know how to teach, but there he was, doing it. I was learning to read. It felt like a kind of miracle to me, like I could do magic, or fly—or be free.

When Stephen was burning the newspaper, he said to me, "Nice flowers on the supper table."

"They're all right," I said. "Just some old summer wildflowers."

"I hear Nick gave them to you."

"Oh, he was just looking for something to do since he wasn't guiding this afternoon."

He was quiet for a minute. Then he said, "Oh. I see now."

I wondered if I needed to feel insulted. Was Stephen thinking Nick was just being nice to me to get back at *him* about the guiding? Like I wasn't good enough for him to be nice to me on his own?

He sort of squared up his shoulders and said, "Would you come in the cave with me tomorrow after the others turn in?"

"For a lesson?"

"No. Not for that. I want to show you something. Something nobody but me's seen yet. I want you to see it next."

"What is it?" I was thinking if it was something like those blind fish, he could just bring it out here. I didn't want to start spending as much time underground as he did. "Can you bring it to me?"

"No. You've got to go there."

"How far inside? More than this?"

"Some. But once you're in here, you're *in* here. You know what I mean? What difference does it make how much more?"

"I like to know how close I am to getting out, that's all."

"As long as you're with me, you can get out. It's something special. You need to see it before anybody else does."

The way he said that to me, I thought maybe he was right. Maybe I did need to see it. So I said, "All right, I will."

He gathered up the lanterns and he was smiling. "Thank you," he said.

"For what?"

"For trusting me. You can, you know."

I did know.

16

THE NEXT NIGHT WE WENT BY OUR LITTLE LESSON ROOM, and kept on going. I looked back at it like I was saying goodbye to an old friend.

We walked on a path for a while, and then we got off it, climbing over some rocks, squeezing through a tight place (scared me to death thinking I could get stuck there), bending round sharp corners, going deeper and deeper in.

It was dark in a way it never got dark outside. No matter how long you waited for your eyes to get used to that dark so you could see something without the lamp, they never would. You *never* could see in there by yourself. And it smelled old. Old and deep, somehow. And quiet, like sounds hadn't been invented yet. Every now and then I had to shiver just thinking on it.

"Are we almost there?" I asked him.

"Almost. When we get near, I want you to close your eyes so I can surprise you."

I was already feeling surprised and not sure how many more surprises I wanted to have. But when he told me to, I shut my eyes, and he took my hand and led me somewhere. Then he said I should stand there while he got something ready. Good thing I trusted him like I did, or I'd have been worrying there was some kind of trick coming my way—like I would have if it was Nick instead of Stephen.

When I finally got to open my eyes, I couldn't believe what I was seeing. We were in a room all white and glittery, and it looked like white and glittery flowers were growing all over—on the walls and the ceiling and some on the floor, too. Or like somebody had just been throwing snowballs all around. Stephen put his two lanterns down on the floor so we had plenty of light, and it just glowed, like being inside stars.

"How did you do this?" I whispered.

"I didn't. God and the cave together, they did it. I just found it like this."

"It doesn't seem real." I kept turning round and round, looking at it all.

"I thought maybe you'd like to write your name on one of these white walls. Maybe here, in this hidden place." He showed me a spot where the glittery wall bent, making a fold that would be hard to see into unless you were holding a lantern right up to it, the way Stephen was doing.

I put my hand on it, and it was rough and scratchy. "How can I write on that?" I wasn't even sure I wanted to. It seemed wrong to make a mark on all that whiteness. But at the same time, I wanted to see how my name looked on what was the prettiest, most amazing thing I'd ever seen.

"You can smoke it on. I brought candles. You know how that tallow smokes. You can do it that way."

I liked that. Smoke seemed a better way to write on that kind of wall than anything else I could think up.

He lit a candle, waited for the smoke, and put it in my hand. I stood for a minute just looking at how it all was before I changed it forever.

Once I did it, I almost wished I hadn't. Almost. My CHARLOTTE looked *so* black against all that white. But maybe that was the way it was supposed to be. Black like me up against so much white that was rough, and scratchy, and great big.

"You want to put your name here, next to mine?" I asked Stephen. "You're the one that found the place."

"No," he said. "This is your place. I'm naming it Charlotte's Grotto. If that's all right with you."

"How can I say it's not all right? This is the best place I've ever seen. I thank you a thousand times for naming it for me. But what will Dr. Croghan think about this place being named for a slave?"

"I'll tell him it's called the Snowball Room. But you and I will have our secret. We'll know its real name."

Not till later did I think about how that room full of magic flowers made Nick's little bunch of wildflowers look pretty puny. I wondered if Stephen had thought of that.

"Years from now," Stephen said, "when folks are still coming to see this cave, they'll come in here, and maybe they'll find your name there and wonder, 'Who *was* this Charlotte, so special to somebody to have her name there?' "

So I was special? That was nice to hear.

"I'm making a map for Dr. Croghan's book, you know."

"A map? Of what?"

"Of everything in here. Now I've got a new place to add. The Snowball Room. The place only you and I will know the real name of."

"You must be changing that map every day, the way you keep finding new places."

"The hardest part is showing how some parts of the cave are lower than other parts. How some paths cross over other paths that are farther down. I need a model, more than a map. But I'm working it out."

I was sure of that. Stephen was the kind of person who, once he started something, he'd see it through to the finish.

"I think I might have found something else real big, too," he told me.

"Better than this?" I pointed all around Charlotte's Grotto.

"Different. I think I found a passage that might go clear across Houchins Valley, all the way over to Flint Ridge Cave. I'm thinking these two caves are really all part of one big cave."

I'd never heard of Houchins Valley or Flint Ridge Cave. "How far you reckon that is?"

"I gauge it about three miles, give or take."

I couldn't credit that any more than I could credit that Charlotte's Grotto had been made by water. "No! A cave three miles across?"

"And longer. A lot longer. We've already got almost twenty miles' worth of cave right here, all winding around. I'm thinking if I keep looking, I can find a way to go from where we're standing right now all the way to the other side of the valley, all inside the caves."

"How do you even know about that other cave? Have you been there?"

"Mr. Gorin took me once. Wanted to show me how much better our cave was than that one. I saw right away how alike they looked inside. But I'd never seen any other caves—I was thinking maybe all caves look the same. Since then, I've had teachers come on my tours and tell me about caves—how there's all different kinds—wet ones, dry ones, plain ones, ones with lots of fancy formations, big ones, little ones, simple ones, complicated ones. I think what we've got here is a big, complicated one."

"Sounds like a long hard trip from here to there."

"Probably is. But then there'll be another way out. That's always a good thing, right?"

"Any way out is good. More than one way is better. You think you'll try going all that way? Alone?"

"Who else?"

"Nick, he'd go with you."

"You think Mr. Miller would let us both be gone for a couple of days? Me, he knows sometimes I'm exploring around for a day or so when there's no tours to lead. Long as he's got an idea when I'll be back, he doesn't worry. I guess if I stayed gone three or four days, he'd have something to say. And if I didn't come back at all, he'd figure I'd run into bad trouble I wasn't coming back from."

"He wouldn't think you'd just run off?"

Stephen shrugged. "He's always let me go in there by myself, and he never tells me when I have to be back unless I have a tour. He knows how I feel about this place, and he knows that most of what I do, I need to do alone. Can't have two guides gone exploring at the same time."

Nick explored, too, but I knew it wasn't the same with him as it was with Stephen. Nick wasn't ever going to make a map. Or find a way to the other side of the valley. Or even really want to. Nick's exploring was more about him than about the cave.

Then I started thinking about a cave so big it went all under a big valley, and was on different levels like floors in a house, and I got a feeling in my stomach almost like I was going to be sick. I was down underneath the ground in a place nobody but me and Stephen even knew was there, and it was too quiet, and too dark, and too strange.

"Stephen," I said, "I've got to go. I've got to get out of here."

"Why? What happened?"

"It's just too much for me to think on, all these dark underground places where folks hear whispers and footsteps, and there's rivers, and bats, and blind fish, and who knows what all else. I need to be up on top where people are supposed to be."

"People can be down here, as well."

"Stephen!" I had to get stern with him, else he'd start trying to convince me why staying down there was something I had to do. "I've got to go up. Now."

He saw I meant it. "All right, all right," he said, a little grumbly. "I keep hoping you'll start to see things down here the way I do—how grand and peculiar this place is."

"It's peculiar, all right. Now let's go."

So he brought me out. It was late, and dark, and real still. Once we were on the top, I didn't forget to tell him how much I liked Charlotte's Grotto, and to thank him for naming it for me.

"I wanted to do something special for you," he said. "Just for you. The things I find down there, they're the most special things I know of. But maybe you don't see it like that."

I wanted to see it like that. For him. 'Cause I knew it was so important, and he had paid me such a big compliment with Charlotte's Grotto. He liked me. And I liked him. Lots more than Nick. I wanted him to keep on liking me. But I was thinking, telling him lies wasn't the best way for us to be starting off. I couldn't have him thinking something was so if it wasn't.

"I do thank you. I do. And I see how much you value everything down there, and I honor that. I'm never going to feel that way about that place, but I honor how you do. And I take it very personal how you like to share it with me. I want you to keep doing that. But I've got to tell you, I'm scared down there, and I'm always going to be. Especially since Delphine talked about seeing and hearing something in there. That's your place, not mine."

"You don't have to be scared about that cave, Charlotte. Delphine, she was just fevered and imagining."

"Maybe I don't *have* to be scared, but I am. And I can tell you, talking to me about it isn't going to change my mind. But hear the other part of what I said. Did you?"

"Yeah. I heard. And I'm going to keep sharing with you. 'Cause I want to. And I'm glad you want me to keep doing it."

"All right, then. That's fine. We understand."

Then he took both my hands in his and just held on to them while he kept looking in my eyes. "You're the most special thing around here, cave or no cave, and I don't want you forgetting I think so."

"That's not the kind of thing a girl's likely to forget," I told him. And my heart was banging away just like it did when I was scared.

So we stood there looking at each other for a while more, and then, still holding hands, we went up the hill to our quarters.

Course the Snowball Room turned into another big success with the visitors, and they all just had to go see it, especially with Stephen guiding. And, as far as I know, not one of them has ever found that hidden place with the word CHARLOTTE on it.

17

STEPHEN AND I WERE ABLE TO MEET IN THE EVENINGS
and go to the cave for a few more lessons without anybody notic-
ing anything out of the ordinary. Anybody but Mittie, that is.

"Ain't we got enough to worry about already without you and
Stephen gettin' together? Nick, he's lookin' like a thunderhead
these days. I'm bettin' it won't be long 'fore he takes it up with
Stephen."

"I can't worry about what Nick might do," I told her. "I've got
my life. True, it's not much, but I get to be the one deciding about
some pieces of it. Not Nick. And what you do mean about Stephen
and me 'getting together'? We're having lessons, that's all. There's
nothing for Nick to take up with Stephen." I wasn't ready yet to
have everybody knowing what was getting started with me and
Stephen—just in case it came to nothing. It was still too new and
tender to be out. One more thing to keep quiet about.

"I ain't lived all these years and learned nothin'," she said, all grumpy. "Maybe I can't read a book, but I can read what's goin' on with you two."

"Which is *nothing*." And I whipped out of that kitchen house like I was late for something important, which I wasn't.

Truly, there wasn't much happening with me and Stephen just then. Oh, I was learning to read, all right. And to write. In fact, I was also learning what Mittie had said was so—that once you knew something, it was hard to pretend you didn't. When I was dusting the main room at the hotel, I wanted to try to read the books there, the ones about the cave, and the newspapers left by the guests. Some of those papers were from far away, and I wanted to read about those other places. I could catch a glimpse of some articles, but I had to keep reminding myself not to look too long. Somebody might notice.

Keeping that secret was lots harder than keeping quiet about the runners. They weren't hardly in my mind at all. We hadn't had one since Delphine, so it was easy to believe there weren't any runners to worry about.

Since Delphine, though, I knew Stephen had been fretting about getting mixed up with another runner. He should have known I wouldn't make him do something he didn't want to do. The way it happened with Delphine was an accident, just 'cause he was there with me when we found her.

One night he was extra quiet going into the cave for our lesson. Usually he liked telling me about what he'd found that day, or what one of his tourists said, but his lips were buttoned that night.

Finally I had to ask him what was his trouble. At first he didn't want to say, just kept mumbling it was nothing, but finally he asked me if I knew what my slave price was. If I knew how much I'd been sold for.

I never had thought about that. Being sold was bad enough by itself. Knowing what somebody else thought you were worth, somebody who didn't even know you, was worse.

"I don't know," I told him. "And I don't want to know. I've got my own value for myself. Why are you asking? Are you being sold?" But that couldn't be. Dr. Croghan knew how much business Stephen brought to the cave. He was making plenty on account of Stephen. He'd never sell him. At least not as long as Stephen was being useful.

"You know I get tips from guiding," he said. "People give me money."

I didn't know that. I'd never known a slave who had any money of his own.

"I've been saving them up in a jar. So a couple days ago I went to count them up. I hadn't done that before, since I haven't got anything to spend them on anyway. And mostly, I don't know what things cost. I never bought much except things for Mr. Gorin's household—tools, or fuel, or food sometimes. You know how much I had? Two hundred and thirty-four dollars. Seems to me that's a lot of money. Enough to buy something big. So I got to thinking, is it enough to buy a person?

"I know Mat and Nick are leased for a hundred dollars a year. How much more would it cost to buy them? And who's worth more—a girl, 'cause she can have babies and make more slaves? Or a strong field hand? Or somebody like Mittie, old and cranky, but a good cook? Or me? What am I worth? Shouldn't God be the one to decide that? Could I buy a slave for two hundred and thirty-four dollars?"

I couldn't keep quiet anymore. "You want to buy yourself a slave? Are you thinking straight?"

"No," he said, looking hard at me. "Not any slave. I wanted to buy me. Myself. From Dr. Croghan."

Oh, mercy, I thought. He doesn't know anything about being a slave. Nothing at all. "You asked him that?"

"I did. I asked him how much to buy me. And he thought somebody else was trying to buy me away from him. He got all up in the air about that. 'Cause I was *his*." Stephen stopped talking and just looked at the ground. Then he said, real quiet, "Aren't I *mine*?"

"Not when you're a slave," I had to tell him.

"So I told Dr. Croghan, no, I wanted to buy myself. And you know what he did?"

"I'm hoping all he did was laugh. 'Cause he could have had you whipped for that."

"He did. He laughed. And he told me I couldn't buy what wasn't for sale. And I shouldn't listen if anybody was talking to me about freedom, since the way I've got it here is better than I could ever have it anywhere else, even if I was free."

"Maybe he's right about how good it is here," I said, "but he doesn't know what it feels like, being owned. He doesn't know how being free's worth something."

"He said he'd free me."

I nearly fell over. "He told you that?"

"He said he'll free me in his will. So I've got to wait till he dies, and then I've got to wait seven more years. Then I'll be free."

I never had heard him talk so bitter. "What do you mean, seven more years?" Having to wait to be free till somebody died was bad enough. Why seven more years?

"He says that's customary when a slave gets freed in some-body's will. That it takes a slave seven years to figure out how to get ready to be free. What do you think about that?"

"I think our Dr. Croghan's got a crack in his head. He doesn't know anything about getting ready to be free. What does he think we're doing now, working like dogs? That's what we'd be doing if we were free, too, except then we'd have a say in where we live, and who we work for, and what we do."

"How can a man keep owning me even after he's dead?" Stephen asked me.

Course I didn't have any answer for that.

Stephen sat up straight then, and he looked right at me and said, "He told Mr. Gorin when he bought me that he'd give me a pass so I could go to Glasgow once in a while to see Mama and Tandy, but he never has. Now I can't even know for sure they're still there. So whatever you need from now on for your runners, I can do it. I know that cave like nobody else. I could hide a hundred runners all at the same time and they wouldn't even know the others were there. You just tell me, 'cause I'll be staying here with this cave as far as I can see. I'll be here to help."

Course I was happy to hear that, and I said thank you, but I could see Stephen still didn't truly understand. When you're a slave, you can't ever say you'll be somewhere for as far as you can see. That's up to somebody else. But Stephen was getting there.

18

I NOTICED THEN, WHILE STEPHEN WAS QUIET AND PRE-occupied (it was starting to look like there wasn't going to be any reading lesson that night), some little sound somewhere I couldn't place.

"Hey, Stephen," I said. "You hear that?"

He tipped his head to listen, and said, "Hear what?"

I put my finger across my lips to shush us both, and we listened. I heard a sort of whisper of sound, like somebody walking real quiet in soft shoes. "There," I breathed. "That."

He listened hard, I could tell, but then he shook his head. "I didn't hear a thing. What did you hear?"

"Sounded like . . . like footfalls. Real little ones."

"Now are *you* going to start hearing ghosts in here?"

I got a little huffy then. "I can't say what I'm hearing is a ghost, but I'm hearing *something*. So I know Delphine wasn't making it up. That noise was real."

He just raised up his eyebrows at me in a way that made me want to whack him.

"Didn't your mama ever talk to you about the spirits?"

"She did some. She even said she'd seen one or two. But I never did. I like to see what I'm believing in."

"Well, I never saw one either, but I believe they're there. Just makes sense to me there's folks who've got unfinished business here they need to keep track of, or there's a person they just miss way too much to leave. Or they somehow got stuck in between and can't move on. Maybe those are the ones in here—the stuck ones. That's maybe why they keep roaming."

It's hard to say why, but hearing those footsteps and thinking about people stuck from moving on made me feel a mite better about being in that cave. I could understand about being stuck and not feeling so good about it. I understood they weren't mean or dangerous—they were just confused.

Stephen handed me a newspaper. "Why don't you read a little? This got left behind by a visitor."

Well, finally! "All right. Let's see." I turned pages, looking for something interesting to read to him. "This article here, it's from Ripley, Ohio. Oh, listen to this! It says, 'Our Town: A Sanctuary for Runaway Slaves?' " I had some trouble with that word "sanctuary" 'cause I never had seen it written out before. But I knew what it meant since I'd heard it in a hymn about how Jesus was ours. And I had to work hard to read the rest of the article, but it was so interesting it kept me going. "It says here this town, Ripley, it's right on the other side of the Ohio River, and Ohio, it's a free state. Once a runner gets over that river, he's supposed to be free. But if he's caught, he can still get sent back to his owner. So some people there, they're hiding the runaways and helping them go on to the next place, as far as Canada. On the Underground Railroad." I looked up at him. "You know what that is?"

He shook his head, but I could see he was interested in anything underground.

"It's not a real railroad. Or really underground," I said. He looked a little disappointed. "It's a secret way of helping slaves run away. Going from one place where they can hide to the next."

He nodded then, but didn't ask any questions, or say anything more about it. Anyway, I'd already told him everything I knew about it, which wasn't much.

So we finished up with reading the article, and then went on out. And all the while I was listening for something that wasn't us. I didn't hear anything, but I thought I could *feel* something. Some presence—and not a scary one. Just a lost one.

Later, I asked Mittie if she knew about the Underground Railroad, and she told me she'd known about it for a long time. And she knew about the places in Ripley, Ohio, too, where her runners could find help if they got that far.

I said, "So we here, could we be part of this railroad?"

"I reckon," she said, bustling, as always, this time kneading bread. "But we're *really* underground." She laughed her raspy laugh at her joke. "But we ain't gonna do that. Too hard to do it regular with all these people around. So far, every runner ended up here's come by accident. I did have to learn where to send them on to. But let's stay out of the regular railroad business."

I pinched myself off a little piece of dough and was making it into a shape. An angel, maybe. "I'm looking for how to help our runners more," I said.

"Now we got a place to hide them, that's a lot more. We can give them rest, and food, and directions to the next safe place, and tell them how to read the quilts other slaves hang out the windows, or on laundry lines or fences."

"Quilts?"

"The patterns on some quilts, they got information and directions. Lucky for us most white folks don't think we got sense enough to figure out such a thing. And it's smart to let them think that. Like that song." And she sang in her cracked old voice, " 'I got one mind for the master to see, and one mind for what I know is me.' "

I'd never heard that song before, but I knew just what it meant.

"We get white folks stayin' here from all over," she went on, "and they got lots to tell each other that I overhear. And their slaves they bring along with them, they talk, too. I learn a lot that way. And us bein' so close to a free state, there's lots of talk about runners and abolition, and like that." She covered the bowls of rising dough and washed her hands.

All I ever heard the traveling slaves talk about was the cave, which Nick and Stephen were happy to tell all about. "Abolition?" I stumbled on that new word. "What's that?"

"It's about stoppin' slavery. Freein' every slave." She dumped a bag of beans into a kettle and poured water over them.

"There's white people who want to do that?" I never knew of anybody—except slaves, naturally—who ever thought that.

"And thank the Lord for 'em, too. Not that I think that will ever happen. But those folks, they's a big help for runners. So I'm hopin' they don't get discouraged." She shook her head and went back to her beans.

I left to tend to the chamber pots up in the hotel with a big new idea in my head—an idea about all slaves getting to be free at the same time. If that ever happened, the only chamber pot I'd have to empty would be my own.

After I'd seen to the pots, I stopped in the main room to straighten up, and got to reading an article in a Chicago newspaper about an actress come to town to be in a play, bringing three little dogs and a bird in a cage with her. I was kind of chuckling over that when I looked up and saw one of the guests, a big, fat man from Atlanta, Georgia, watching me.

"You readin' that paper, girl?" he asked me.

I dropped it like it was on fire. "No, sir. How could I do that? I was just lookin' at the picture."

He came across that room like he was on wheels, and took up that paper. "There's no picture on this page," he said.

I pointed at a little drawing on the bottom of the page showing the bird in his cage, but I was scared to say any more.

Then he raised that paper and hit me across the face with it so hard, and so unexpected, I went down on my knees. "Don't you go gettin' any ideas, girl." And he took that paper with him and left.

I stayed down for a minute, holding my face and catching my breath. Mittie was sure right. Once you knew something, it was hard to remember to pretend you didn't.

19

STEPHEN WAS ALL RUFFLED THE NEXT NIGHT AT SUPPER because of something that had happened in the cave that day with one of his tours. I was serving, so I was missing the story he was telling Mittie, Nick, and Mat, except for what I could patch together in pieces. But after, when we were cleaning up, he was still telling it.

"I've never been that scared before in there," he said. "Even when I get myself in a tight fix exploring, not knowing if I'm going over the edge of some big pit or getting stuck in some close tunnel, I know I always have myself to depend on."

I handed him some bowls to put away. "All 'cause of something some man said to you?"

"When I'm guiding, I'm the boss," he said. "Those tourists, they've got to do what I say. I tell them it's to keep them safe 'cause I know that place in a way they never can. And they believe me. Especially once they get in there, and see how big, and how dark, and how peculiar it is. Once in a while, there's some man talking smart about 'How hard can it be?' but inside, he usually quiets down.

"This time I had me a family from Atlanta, Georgia. Big loud father, timid mama, bunch of kids wanting to run off in all directions. I kept speaking to them, saying how they might end up spending a day or two all alone in the dark if they got away from the group and it took us some time finding them. But those little buggers, they weren't listening to me. Finally I just said I was going to teach them a lesson so they'd know what it would be like to be lost in there. And I blew out my lantern, and walked away, making sure they could hear my feet going off."

Mittie was shaking her head while she washed up some cups, 'cause she knew what was coming and I didn't. Mat and Nick shook their heads along with her.

"You didn't," I said. I was getting a kind of sick feeling in my stomach, thinking about being in there alone in the dark with who I thought that man was.

"I didn't get more than a few steps off before you never heard such caterwauling in your life. All those kids were crying, and the mama, too, and the father, he was just plain yelling, calling me all kinds of names—things I can't say in front of you. And I was getting a feeling like I'd made a bad mistake, forgetting how he's white and I'm not, the way it's easy to do when I'm down there, and with the way the light is, we all look the same color. I might have forgot, but he didn't."

Oh, Stephen, I thought. That's something you shouldn't ever forget.

"So I got that lantern lit up again in a hurry, and the caterwauling stopped except for the father, who was still hopping mad—mostly, I'm guessing, 'cause he'd been as scared as everybody else, and maybe more."

"Then what happened?" I asked, drying the same platter over and over till it squeaked.

"Well, he couldn't rightly kill me, or he knew they'd never get out of there, so he hit me hard on the back of my head, and yelled at me the rest of the way on the tour, and told Mr. Miller about it when we got back. Made it sound like I'd tried to kill them all."

"What did Mr. Miller do?" That platter kept squeaking.

"Charlotte," Mittie hollered at me, exasperated, "will you put that platter down 'fore you make me deaf!"

I put it and my towel down on the table. "What did Mr. Miller do?" I asked again.

"He dressed me down good while that man stood there, and he told him I'd be punished. Once that man left us, he was still pretty mad, but mostly he said don't do it again."

"Were you afraid you'd get whipped?" I asked.

"I wondered about it, but I've never seen Mr. Miller do anything like that, so I wasn't too worried."

"You got to watch your mouth," Mittie said. "And your mind. Or you're goin' to have more trouble with more visitors. You been lucky so far, bossin' them around. Be better if you could joke them around like Nick."

Nick smiled to himself, carrying a stack of plates to a shelf.

Stephen's mouth set itself in a hard line, and then he said, "I have my joking times with them. But that cave's not a joke, and I want my visitors to see that. I know Nick likes guiding, and he likes the cave, but he doesn't *study* it the way I do. He doesn't *know* it the way I do. He doesn't *treat* it the way I do. I can't be Nick."

Nick had his back to Stephen, but I could see his smile change to a frown.

Mittie must have been paying enough attention to know how much competing went on between Stephen and Nick. What was she trying to do, make it worse? Or maybe just trying to get Stephen to pay attention to something important.

It didn't work, though. All Stephen did was put down his towel, and the cup he was drying, and disappear out the door. Which wasn't like him. Not at all.

We finished our cleaning up in silence. After Nick and Mat had gone off to their horseshoes, I said to Mittie, "He doesn't like being compared to Nick. Don't you know that?"

"I'm tryin' to get him to be sensible," she said. "And not think he's somethin' special just 'cause he knows his way around some cave."

"He *is* something special. He explores in there all by himself, which is harder than you can imagine, especially since you've never been in there. And he makes discoveries that get written about in the newspapers, and he knows about geology, and Greek myths, and he can read and write . . ."

"And he's still a slave," Mittie said, drying her hands. "It don't matter how smart you get if somebody else owns you. Nick, he can explore, too, but he never forgets he's a slave, like Stephen does. Now, take this dishwater and dump it."

I dumped the water out the back door, and then went on to bed. There wasn't any light showing in Stephen's window. He must have gone back inside that cave—where he felt the most free.

We had another runner that night. Mittie found him when she got up, still in the dark, to get the fire going for baking the day's bread. She came and woke me, and we went for Stephen to hide him. I was fearful Stephen'd still be inside the cave, but he was asleep in his bed, thank the Lord.

He shooed Mittie and me out while he put on his pants, and then he took our runner—Marshall was his name—into the cave, quick, before any of our visitors, or Mr. Miller, were stirring.

"How'd he seem with it?" I asked Stephen at breakfast.

"He was so weary, he was just glad to be able to lie down and sleep," Stephen said. "He's got lanterns, and food, and blankets— he'll do fine."

"Good thing Mittie found him when she did. Before the sun came up and anybody could have spotted him. Every runner gives me a new way to be scared."

Then I had to start carrying trays of food up to the hotel dining room, serving breakfast to that man from Atlanta like I didn't know one thing about him.

20

THAT NIGHT, AFTER EVERYTHING WAS QUIET AT THE HOTEL and on the grounds, we went into the cave to take Marshall some food and some lamp oil—but mostly I just wanted to have some time with Stephen.

Marshall was glad to see us, for sure, but he also wasn't in any hurry to get out, which surprised me.

"Bein' in here's the safest I ever been," he said. "My whole life before, seems like I was always waitin' for somethin' bad to happen. And it just about always did. I been whipped more times than I can count—and most times I didn't even know why. So yeah, I'm likin' it in here. Plenty of food, rest, and quiet—long as I don't mind the footsteps and the talkin'."

"You mean the tour groups?" Stephen asked. But the way he said it, I could tell he knew that wasn't what Marshall meant.

"Groups?" Marshall asked. "Sounded like but one or two."

"Could you hear what they were saying?" Stephen asked.

Marshall scratched his head. "It's loud enough, but I can't understand them. It's some other kind of language, I'm thinkin'. But they's just talkin', not fightin' or nothin'."

So Marshall thought there were a couple of strangers walking around in the cave speaking a foreign language, did he? I gave Stephen a look, but he just shook his head at me, a quick little jerk.

On our way out, I said, "I think those spirits in there are looking out for our runners. Kind of keeping an eye on them, keeping them company. They know how it is to be in between places. Can't go back, not sure where they're going next."

Stephen set his jaw real stiff, and he said, "I've never heard any spirits in my cave. You and Marshall—"

"—and Delphine—"

"—and Delphine—the three of you are just nervous in here. You scare yourselves into hearing things."

"You'll see," I told him. "One of these days you'll see. Your mama's right. There is such a thing as spirits, and they aren't all out just to make mischief."

"You and me, we're going to have to disagree about that, that's what," he said. "It's water dripping, or echoes from the tours, or Mat's harmonica, for all I know. But it's not ghosts." And then he turned to me and took both my hands in his. "But I'm glad I'm helping you with the runners. I'm scared of being caught, and I'm scared of you being caught—I'm pretty much scared most of the time—but I still know it's the right thing."

I squeezed his hands. "Everything you're saying is true. And I'm glad you're in on it. I don't like having to keep secrets from you. I've got enough I have to keep from everybody else."

"I don't want you thinking you have to keep things from me. I want you to tell me anything. We haven't got much we can hang on to in this world. I want to hang on to you."

My stomach was doing little flip-flops when he said that. "You can," I said. "If you let me hang on to you."

"I'll more than let you," he said. "I'll beg you to." And then he turned loose my hands, and he put his arms around me, and he kissed me.

I'd heard people talk about kissing, and I'd kissed my mama a few times on the cheek, but this kiss was something new, like a thing I'd never even heard of before. I felt it all over. Not just on my lips. Everything seemed more—well, I don't know what. Just *more*. I could have stayed down in that cave forever, just kissing Stephen and feeling those new feelings.

He stopped kissing me, and lifted up his head, and looked me in the eyes for a long time, not saying a word. And then he kissed me again, which saved me the trouble of thinking what to say about this.

When he finally quit kissing me, the only thing I could say was "Oh."

"Are you mad?" Stephen asked me. "Are you mad I did that?"

"No!" I said, too loud. And then I had to laugh. "No," I said, softer. "I'm glad you did it. I've been wondering if you thought about it."

"I've been thinking about it for the longest time, afraid you were finding Nick more to your liking."

"Nick? Oh, no. He hasn't got a serious bone in him. I like that you're serious, that you think about things, and wonder about things, and that you're an abolitionist." I wanted to show him that I thought about things, too.

"I'm a what?" He held me a little ways off and frowned at me.

"An abolitionist. Somebody who believes there shouldn't be slavery at all. That every slave should be free at the same time, so there wouldn't be any need for running away, or hiding, or selling families apart."

"Well, if that's what it means, then I guess I am one of those. But so's every other slave. And what good does it do? We've still got no say."

"But there's white folks who think that way. *They*'ve got a say. Maybe they'll make it happen."

"I'm not holding my breath for that day," he said. "I want to have things as good as I can have them *now*, not wait forever for them. That's why I did this." And he kissed me once more.

I wasn't sure I'd ever get used to the feeling of being kissed, but I was already not so surprised by it. Once Stephen got started, it seemed like he didn't care to stop. Finally I had to back up.

"Is this going to be another secret we've got to keep?" I asked.

"Only if that's how you want it. I want to tell everybody that I love Charlotte Brown and she's my girl."

Nobody had ever said they loved me before. Mama did love me, I knew that, but she never said it. Sally and the boys, well, maybe. They were my sister and brothers, after all, but we never thought that way. So to hear Stephen say it, somebody who wanted me for his own—well, it was the best feeling I ever had.

"Say that again," I told him. My ears couldn't get enough.

He laughed, but he did it. And then he said it one more time.

"I don't expect I'll ever get tired of hearing that," I said. "And I don't care who knows we're together. I'm just happy we are."

That feeling lasted even when we passed by one of the hotel guests out for a late cigar on the path down to the cave mouth. Lucky we smelled that cigar in time to stop talking about our runner. He didn't say a word to us, but seeing him there reminded us how easy getting caught could be. But for once my fear wasn't big enough to drown how happy I was.

21

IT DIDN'T TAKE MITTIE LONG TO FIGURE OUT SOMETHING was changed between me and Stephen. By the next morning at breakfast she knew.

"So Stephen finally said somethin' to you," she said when she and I were alone in the kitchen house, getting the breakfasts started.

"What are you talking about?" I said. But I knew.

"A cow could see how crazy he is about you. Nick sure wasn't missin' it. And it was makin' him cranky. Least maybe he'll settle down now the battle's over."

"Battle? There was a battle?"

"Not one out in the open," Mittie said, cracking eggs in a bowl. "But it was there, just waitin' for you to make your pick."

"You think so?"

"Don't tell me you hadn't already decided you liked Stephen better'n Nick."

"What if I did? I still had to wait. There's good interest, and there's bad interest, and you don't always know which one it is that's coming your way. I needed to know what kind before I was thinking about picking."

"So Stephen let you know."

"Yes. He did. And it's the good kind. The same kind I've got for him."

She stopped beating the eggs and just stood, looking at me. But it seemed she was also looking at something far away in her memory. "Well, you're lucky," she said. "Enjoy it as long as you can. It don't always last."

"Did you love somebody once?" I asked her. I'd never have had the nerve if she hadn't had that far-off look.

She nodded. "But he got sold away." She sighed, and picked up the whisk again. "And there was never anybody else like him," she went on, brisk as ever. "So you make your memories now."

"I will," I said, but I felt like a big dark cloud had gone over the sun. Why couldn't I just be happy for a while without somebody scaring me about how it could all come to an end?

We got Marshall moved on in a couple of days, and I started thinking maybe we were done with runners for a while. That thought made my heart feel lighter. The summer was finishing up. The nights were getting chilly even while the daytime was still warm, and we were getting a lot of rain. Rainy days weren't good for runners, and they weren't good for visitors, either. The rainwater seeped down into the cave and flooded some passages, and made the underground rivers overflow. Yes, there was more than just the River Styx now. Stephen had found another one. He called it Echo River. Mr. Miller had a new rule, ever since a visitor had almost got caught in an underground flood. He wouldn't let anybody, not even Stephen, go in the cave when it was raining. Too dangerous and too unpredictable.

So we stayed in our cabins resting and listening to the rain. I'd fixed my room up with dried flowers, and pretty rocks, and pinecone arrangements, and it really felt like my own little home. Or we hung around the kitchen house. The boys played cards, Mittie cooked, and usually I ironed or mended—jobs that never did seem to get finished.

Staying out of the cave was hard for Stephen. When he wasn't guiding, he wanted to be in there exploring. Rainy days made him restless and jumpy. One dreary wet afternoon when we were all in the kitchen house, Stephen kept coming to hang over me where I was working, then over to Mittie to taste what she was cooking, then back to the card table where Mat waited patiently for him, and Nick didn't.

"Come on, Stephen," Nick said. "Leave the ladies alone. We got some cards to play here. And that cave's goin' to be fine for a while without you. Settle down and deal."

"I can't," Stephen said. "This weather's making me fidgety. I'm going outside."

"Outside? Are you crazy?" Nick asked. "It's pouring. And it's cold."

"Can't help it," Stephen said. "It's too close in here for me." And out he went into the downpour.

We had just a couple of visitors then, hopeful ones waiting for the rain to stop, so Mittie didn't have much cooking, and I didn't have many chamber pots. In fact, we were starting to wonder what we'd be doing that winter, since there wouldn't be all the building and organizing going on that there'd been the winter before. We were talking about how maybe Nick and Mat might be going back to Nashville to their owner. Nick was saying I'd be welcome to come along with them, it'd make the winter pass fast, when Stephen came bursting back in the kitchen-house door, dripping wet all over. Mittie gave him one of her crossest looks, and started in on him. "What you doin' in here gettin' my whole floor wet?"

But he just stared at her and said, "There's a girl and her baby out there in this."

Mat and Nick took one look at each other and got up from the table. "We'll be seeing you all at suppertime," Nick said, and the two of them left. Through the window I could see them running through the rain down to their cabins.

"Put them in my cabin," Mittie said. "I don't like doing that, but we got no choice right now. They'll have to wait till after the supper's been served and cleared up to get in the cave. Be quick. Shouldn't be nobody out and around in this weather, but you never can know what white people will do."

"I'll go, too," I said, putting down my mending. I pulled my shawl up over my head and ran out with Stephen.

He took me down by the cave where, huddled inside the bushes, was a girl looking younger than me, hugging this baby close to her chest, the both of them soaked through what little they were wearing, and shivering. I put my hands on the girl and said, "You've got to come with us. And be quick."

She didn't say a thing. Just got up and came, hanging on tight to that baby, and sticking a lot closer to me than to Stephen. We got her to Mittie's and all of us pushed inside, breathing like bellows. If Mittie was upset about Stephen dripping on her kitchen floor, she was going to have a fit about the four of us dripping in her room.

"We've got to get you out of those wet things," I said to the mama, hoping she could hear me over her teeth chattering. "And the baby, too. What's his name?"

"She's a girl. Name of Primrose. But I call her Primmy."

"That's a sweet name," I said, pulling the blanket off Mittie's bed. There were two more under it still on the bed. She'd been making use of the hotel linen cupboard, I could see that. And three blankets at the end of summer—she must have had some cold old bones.

I wrapped the blanket around her and told her to get her wet clothes off. But she just kept looking over my shoulder at Stephen, who I'd forgotten all about.

"I'll take care of this," I told him. "You go on back. Us girls'll be all right for now."

"You sure?"

I didn't know how I could say I was. Nothing was sure when we were doing what we were. But I said, "Go."

After he left, it was easier getting Primmy and Venture—that turned out to be the mama's name—wrapped up warm and tucked into Mittie's bed. "I'm going to get you something to eat," I said, "and then you can sleep awhile."

"You sure it's safe?" she said. "Can't remember when I could sleep without worryin'."

I couldn't tell her she could quit worrying, and I didn't want to say she should worry more, so I just left her to run up to the kitchen house. The rain was slowing down, but behind it a little hint of coming fall stayed in the air. The hotel grounds were still deserted, which was good.

Mittie had a basket all ready, so I grabbed it, turned around, and left with it, thinking hard for an excuse why I had it in case I ran into Mr. Miller. I didn't, which was good, 'cause I never came up with anything that made sense.

While I was watching Venture nurse the baby, and eat some bread and rabbit stew, she told me she'd run the night before she was going to be sold off, away from Primmy. She was so scared, she just grabbed Primmy, and nothing else, and went.

"I know they're both after me," she said. "My new owner, and the old one. They're both mad. The one 'cause he ain't got me, and the other 'cause he ain't got the money from sellin' me. They came after me with dogs, I heard them. I walked a long way in a creek. I been told they can't smell you in water. But I don't know if I walked far enough that way."

"The rain helps," I told her, hoping that was true. I didn't want to worry her more, when she was already too thin, and had shadows under her eyes from no sleep and from being too scared. "You two sleep now. After we finish tonight at the hotel we'll come move you to where it's safer."

I hoped we could get that done before any dogs showed up. I surely didn't like the sound of that. Especially now that I had the scent of our runners on me.

22

Back at the kitchen house, I told Stephen and Mittie Venture's story, and warned them that there could be dogs.

"Oh, I hate them dogs," Mittie said. "I got me a bunch of tricks to use with them, but sometimes they're smarter than they look. It's easier to fool a man than a dog."

After we got supper cleaned up, and Mat and Nick had made themselves scarce, Stephen, Mittie, and I went to Mittie's quarters, where Venture and Primmy were curled together in the bed, sound asleep. It had stopped raining, but it was chilly and mighty muddy.

Mittie ran her fingers across Venture's forehead real soft till Venture opened her eyes.

"Shh, shh, sugar," Mittie whispered. "It's just us, comin' to put you in a safer place. Don't you fret none. Let's see if we can get it done without wakin' up this pretty baby of yours."

I'd never heard Mittie talk like that to anybody. It was a big surprise to me—and got me wondering if Mittie herself had had a baby sometime way back.

We got Venture dressed again in her ragged clothes that had dried out while she was sleeping, and wrapped Primmy up tight in some towels from the hotel.

"You know, don't you," Mittie said to Venture, "babies don't cry when they're wrapped up real snug."

"She don't cry much anyways," Venture said. "She's a good baby."

"I know that," Mittie told her. "And I'm givin' you this sugar-teat for her just in case she ever does get to fussin'. It'll be easier for both of you. And this here shawl is for you. I got extras from all the ones the visitors leave behind. Now Stephen, he's our expert on hidin' places, and he's goin' to take you to a good one and get you settled in there. And I'm goin' to take our breakfast ham and rub out where you walked, just in case we get us some dogs here."

"Our ham!" Stephen exclaimed. "I was counting on a piece of that."

"And you'll be gettin' it," Mittie said. "I'll be washin' it off and cookin' it up, and there won't be no evidence at all." She cackled her laugh, the one we hardly ever got to hear.

Venture nodded, and stood up, Primmy still clutched close to her bony chest. Stephen and I left Mittie and led Venture and Primmy down to the mouth of the cave in the damp dark, listening hard for anybody out and about who might come upon us.

"Oh," Venture whispered when we reached the cave mouth. "What's that?"

"That's the best hiding place in the world," Stephen said in a quiet voice. "We've had other runners in there, lying low for a few days till they could move on. Haven't had any complaints yet."

"But where's it go?" she asked.

"Well, it's a cave," Stephen said. "So it goes under the ground."

"Oh, no," she said. "I ain't takin' my little Primmy down there in the dark."

"When we get all the lanterns lit, it won't be dark at all. You'll see."

After everything she'd been through running, didn't she know how dangerous it was for all of us to be standing around discussing right near a hotel full of white people, with dogs maybe on the way? Stephen was sounding patient and calm, but I wanted to push her right on into the cave.

Still Venture hung back. "Is this the only way out?" she asked.

"I don't think so," Stephen said. He put his hand on my arm, like he could feel me about to do something.

"You don't *think* so? I got to know." Venture—worn-out and on the run—was standing up to Stephen like she had all the time in the world.

"I'll get you out," Stephen said. "Nobody knows this cave the way I do."

Her bottom lip came out. "I ain't gettin' trapped again while I'm runnin' away from another trap."

Stephen was finally getting exasperated, I could see that. He took a deep breath and said, "There is another way out. It ends up on the other side of this valley, maybe three miles away. It'd be a long walk, but it's there. And if you need to go out that way, I'll take you."

"All right, then." Venture squared up her shoulders and followed Stephen right into that dark hole, and I came along behind, sweat coming down the back of my dress like it was a midsummer day.

We got Venture and Primmy settled in the little rock room with pillows, and blankets, and lots of lanterns. She seemed all right about it.

"You know," she told me, "I got to be strong for Primmy. She can taste in my milk if I'm scared, so I can't be. I never thought I'd want a baby when I'm just fifteen, but she changed everythin' for me. She's why I'm runnin'. How you like that?"

"I think you're both brave," I said. "Now you get some sleep, and we'll be back tomorrow with more food."

I could hear Venture starting to sing to Primmy as Stephen and I left them.

"You sure they won't get any water in there?" I asked Stephen.

"They're a long way from the rivers. They won't have any problems."

"Did you mean it? That there's another way out? I thought you just *thought* there was."

"I know it's there. Just 'cause I haven't been all the way to the end, I still know for sure it's there. I know this cave."

"But what if you have to take somebody out that way? You don't know for sure you can. What if there's a river in the way? What if—"

"I can do it," he said, real firm. So I knew enough to shut up then. But I still was thinking about Venture and Primmy, about getting them free. Maybe it was 'cause of the baby they were affecting me so. Little Primmy had a chance to remember nothing but freedom. Not like the other runners, who'd always remember how it was being a slave first, before they got free.

Suddenly Stephen stopped and put his lantern down. I did the same. "Look here," he said. "Here's the two of us alone. What do you think we should do about it?" And he held out his arms to me.

23

NICK WAS QUIET THE NEXT MORNING AT BREAKFAST. Course Mat was always quiet, but it seemed like even he was *more* quiet than usual. I knew they didn't want to talk 'cause they didn't want to take any chances on having us tell them something about our runners.

Having secrets, even from somebody who knows you got secrets, is a hard business. They say they don't want to know, and they believe that, but there's a part of them that really does want to know. And you don't want to tell, but at the same time you do. 'Cause a secret is a heavy thing. My secret about reading and writing would have been heavier if there'd been more things to tempt me to read. But my runners, they were a heavy secret now. Especially that baby. I just about had to keep my hand over my own mouth to not say something about Venture and Primmy, even when I was talking to Mittie or Stephen.

As soon as they finished breakfast, Mat and Nick were out of there, ready to take the few tourists we had on a tour together. It was Nick's turn to lead the tour, but Mr. Miller said Mat could go, too, because two guides were better than one, unless you were Stephen. Nick didn't much like hearing that.

Mittie went off to her quarters to rest, so Stephen and I were alone.

"You think Venture might be our last runner this year?" he asked. "Summer's about over. It's starting to get cold." I could hear how much he hoped we wouldn't be hiding anybody else in his cave for a good long while.

"I can't say. If she is, what do you think we'll be doing this winter?" More than anything, I wanted to stay on where I was.

"I've been waiting for Dr. Croghan to come tell us. I want to be here. Winter's a good time for exploring. And there needs to be a guide here just in case of a visitor."

"That means Mittie gets to stay, to cook for whoever comes. You think Mat and Nick will stay?"

"Don't see why. One guide's enough. And there isn't much else for them to do."

"What about me?"

He put his hand on mine. "I hope you'll be here. With me."

"I wish it was up to you. What if Dr. Croghan wants to sell me? Or lease me out for the winter?"

"I hope that doesn't happen."

"Maybe I should just go with Venture when she and Primmy take off. I could help her with the baby."

I don't know why I said that, except I was fearing getting sold again with the winter coming on, and I was affected by how much Venture was willing to do to get free. And maybe I just plain wanted to hear Stephen say again how much he needed me to stay with him.

"You mean that? You really want to go? I thought you and me . . ."

I looked down at our clasped hands. "We are. I mean, I think we are. But getting free—don't you want that? Isn't that more important than anything? I know, I know, we talked about it already, and I see how you feel about that cave, but there's got to be other caves. You could come with us. We could all go together." I was pushing, I knew it. Pushing him to make me stay.

He was quiet for a long time and then he said, "I can't leave. I know you don't understand, but I can't."

"I truly don't. What happens if I *need* to go? Would you pick me or that cave?"

"Don't ask me that," he said. "It's like asking your mama which of her children she likes best."

I took my hand out from under his. "I want to be the child you like best."

He stood and put his hand out to me, but I moved to where he couldn't reach me. "Please, Charlotte. If you stay here with me, you can help a lot of other runners."

"You ever think I might get tired of helping others do what *I* want to do?" I was scaring myself then, digging myself into a hole I didn't want to be in, but there I was. I wanted to hear him say I had to stay for *him*, not to help other runners.

"I can't make you stay if you don't want to," he said. "But being here at the cave, it's a good place for you, and for us both. The work, it's not too hard, and we're good at it. And we can be together."

"Just till one of us gets sold. You've been sold once. Just 'cause you got to stay here doesn't mean it's different now. Don't you see? You're not *free*!"

He took a long breath. "I'm free enough. For me. For now."

"What if I'm not?"

He looked down at his hands on top of the table. "Then you're the one that has to make a choice."

My heart was beating so hard it hurt me. I couldn't think what to say, so I turned and went out the door and to my cabin. I lay on my bed and cried and cried at what I'd done. I'd taken my choices away from myself. I still wanted both, the same as Stephen did.

The next two nights I went in the cave with Stephen, tending to Venture and Primmy, but there weren't any sweet stops on the way out, with just the two of us. In fact, we hardly talked at all.

Nick, as usual, picked up on something between me and Stephen, and he stepped right in between us. Seemed like wherever I went, Nick was there, handing me the clothespins when I hung the wash, helping haul the water and chop the wood, ready to fold sheets when they came off the line, and talking the whole time, telling jokes and stories about his tourists, untying my apron behind my back, making funny faces till I had to laugh.

And Stephen saw it all. But he didn't do one thing to stop it. I was thinking I really might as well go with Venture, since there wasn't much to stay around here for.

I was thinking that the day Mr. Miller and Dr. Croghan both got us gathered in back of the hotel to talk to us. Dr. Croghan started the talking, nothing but business, as usual. "We have two things to talk about today. First, the arrangements for the winter. The Almanac says we're going to have a hard one this year, long and cold and wet, so I'm not expecting we'll have a lot of visitors, though there are always the odd ones who'll come no matter what. We'll need only one guide, so Stephen, you'll stay here, and Mat and Nick will go back to Nashville until the spring."

I saw Nick frown and shoot a sharp look at Stephen, who wasn't paying any attention to him.

"Mittie stays here—we always need a cook—and Charlotte will come to Louisville with me to work at Locust Grove."

Later Mittie told me Locust Grove was the name of Dr. Croghan's house, but I didn't know that then, and I was scared about going to some unknown place.

"If she's needed here from time to time, we can arrange for that. That's all I have to say. Now Mr. Miller has to talk to you."

Dr. Croghan went back inside the hotel, and Mr. Miller started talking before I was ready to listen. I was still worrying about what Locust Grove would be like. But what he said stopped that, and got me to paying attention again.

"It's possible that a runaway slave is hiding somewhere around here. Two men arrived this morning looking for her. They had some trouble tracking her because of the rain, but their dogs have picked up her scent near here. They're not sure if she's still here, or if she's gone on. She has a child with her. Nobody knows this cave better than you three, Stephen, Mat, and Nick. And you, Mittie and Charlotte, you're around the grounds all the time. You must tell me if you've seen her, or anything unusual."

Stephen spoke right up. "No, sir. I haven't seen a thing. And I'd sure notice anything suspicious. I wouldn't take kindly to somebody using our cave for something like that."

"I appreciate that, Stephen. I know how much you value Mammoth Cave, and how hard you work to enhance its reputation. The last thing we'd want is for runaways to begin using our cave as a hiding place."

"Oh, no, sir," Stephen said emphatically. "We surely wouldn't want that."

He was a good liar. Especially for somebody who didn't have much practice at it. Like Mittie always said, white people think we're so stupid it's easy to fool them. Even though Mr. Miller knew Stephen was smart about the cave, he must have thought he was thickheaded about everything else.

Mr. Miller went on, "They're staying tonight. Maybe tomorrow night, too. They mean to find her. How about you, Nick? Mat?"

Mat just shook his head. Nick said, "I don't know nothin' about no runaway. Seems kind of stupid to run to a place that's full of people."

"Well, I don't think runaways have the most sense," Mr. Miller said. "So if you notice anything, you let me know. In the meantime, Nick and Mat, I want you to make up some kind of pen for those dogs. And Stephen, you get ready to take them into the cave."

He turned to go and then turned back. "I'm sure I don't need to tell you what happens to anyone who helps runaways," he said, examining each of our faces.

We all shook our heads and said, "No, sir"—but my head wasn't all that was shaking.

While Nick and Mat went off to build the pen, Stephen and I went into the kitchen house with Mittie.

"They'll find her," Stephen said. "I could lead the men in the wrong direction, but I can't fool the dogs. What am I going to do?"

Mittie handed him a little bag. "Put that in your pocket," she told him.

"What is it?"

"It's red pepper. You need to throw that around inside there so's those dogs can't smell Venture and Primmy. So's they can't smell nothin' but that pepper."

"Will that work?"

"For now it'll work. But men like that, they don't leave off easy. If they have to go home empty-handed, they'll be hirin' bounty hunters to keep lookin' for her. Even if she gets herself to a free state, they can still bring her back. Even if it's years from now. She's got to go all the way to Canada. We got to tell her that's where she can be truly safe. And she's got to know she can never come back."

"Why would she come back?" Stephen asked.

Mittie lifted her bony shoulders. "Some do. They can get to

feelin' too lucky when they don't get caught. Like they *can't* get caught. They come back for somebody they had to leave behind, some family. And sometimes it works. But gettin' out one time is hard enough. Lucky enough. Miracle enough. More than that . . ." She just shook her head.

Then Mr. Miller called for Stephen and he had to go.

I looked out the open window and saw these two big men with dogs on long leads. I was expecting bloodhounds, but these were ordinary mongrel-looking farm dogs. But they had busy noses, twitching in the air, snuffling on the ground, going up and down the men's pant legs where they'd probably wiped their hands after lunch.

I saw Stephen take a deep breath, touch his pocket where the pepper was, and then move to meet them.

"You got somebody hiding in that cave?" one of the men asked Stephen.

"No, sir," Stephen said. "It'd be a bad place to hide. No light. No food. It's cold in there, and uncomfortable. And scary, to most folks."

"None of that means nothing," the other man said. "I pulled one out of a manure pile once. Another one was hiding in a chicken coop, and that's just a different kind of manure pile."

"Yes, sir," Stephen said, while I was thinking about how desperate you'd have to be to hide in a manure pile, and wondering if I'd ever be able to do that, no matter how desperate I was.

"These dogs think something's in that cave. We need to go in and see what they can find."

"Lots of different folks been in and out of this cave for a long time," Stephen said. "No telling what your dogs got the scent of."

"Well, let's go in and find out." And then they all headed down to the cave entrance. If I'd been Stephen, I don't think I'd have been able to take a single step without falling down from fear.

24

"COME AWAY FROM THAT WINDOW," MITTIE SAID TO ME, "and help me here with stringin' these beans."

I sat and stringed beans with her, but we didn't talk. All we did was wait and listen. And then we cooked, and I went up to the hotel to fix the tables for supper, still waiting for Stephen. I thought about Venture and Primmy in their little rock room, not knowing that those men with their dogs were in there looking for them. I thought about Stephen under the ground with men who hated slaves, who were bigger than him, and who had dogs they could put on him if he crossed them. I thought about Mat and Nick, who knew we were hiding a runner, even if they didn't quite know where she was. Would they tell if they were scared enough? I swear, I was dropping silverware all over the floor and having trouble folding napkins with my shaky hands.

Stephen brought the men back just before supper, but because Nick and Mat were with us then in the kitchen house, I couldn't ask him anything about their search of the cave. When Mat and Nick and I carried the platters of fried chicken and greens and potatoes up to the dining room, the men and their dogs were there, taking up a whole table while our other few guests stayed away from them.

After Mat and Nick set down their platters on the buffet and went back to the kitchen house, leaving me in the dining room to serve, I stayed near the men's table, hoping I might hear them talking about what had happened in the cave. But they didn't talk at all. They just ate like they'd never see food again, and I knew I'd be having a hard time getting out the stains of the food they slopped on the tablecloth and the napkins. They fed those dogs off their own plates, and then took them to sleep in their room, so Nick and Mat had built that pen for nothing. And the dogs were getting better treatment from those men than Venture ever had from anyone.

It wasn't until the tables were cleared and Mittie had sent Nick and Mat off for horseshoes, leaving the washing up to Stephen and me, that I got to hear anything about that trip into the cave.

"Did the pepper work?" Mittie asked.

"Not so well," Stephen said. "It was hard to throw it with Jack and Harlan around—that's their names. The dogs didn't like it when I could throw it, that's for sure, and they seemed confused by it. But they still kept getting closer and closer to where Venture and Primmy were. I was getting plenty worried."

"What did you do?" I asked.

Mittie put her hand on my arm to quiet me.

"I was racking my brains for how to stop them, and then I

knew. We were carrying only the one lantern, mind, since they had the dogs to worry about holding on to. So I went a little ways ahead—you know how fast it gets dim in there with just one lantern—and when I was where they couldn't see me clear, I blew it out." He laughed then. "You should have heard them. They sounded like little girls, all skittish. The only word they could say was 'Light! Light!' Even the dogs got jumpy, winding their ropes around their legs and all. Then Harlan, he got mad.

"He was yelling at me to relight the lantern, and I kept saying how it was hard to do in the dark. I was realizing, though, that I would have to relight the lantern and stand by while they found Venture and Primmy and dragged them out. And then I knew I couldn't do that. I knew I'd have to fight them, even if I was sure I'd lose, and I knew what they'd do to me later, once I got them out of the cave.

"Then while I was trying to relight that lantern, I heard this noise, this crazy-sounding, high, echoing kind of shriek. It kept going on and on, and I couldn't locate where it was coming from. I'll tell you, my heart about stopped. Jack and Harlan weren't even able to make words anymore. They were whimpering like babies. So were the dogs. Then, all of a sudden, just when I got the lamp lit again, it stopped. You never heard quiet so quiet. I could hear my own heart beating, and I can promise you, it was going fast. That lantern light never seemed so little. All Jack and Harlan wanted was to get out of there. And me, too. I was wondering by then if there *was* something living down there besides crickets and those blind fish."

"I told you," I said. "There's spirits down there. They're watching out. Then what happened?"

"I don't know about spirits," Stephen said. "But we got ourselves straightened up and headed for the outside, and then that sound started up again. But this time it was lower, a kind of moan that got louder and then softer, and then louder again. It sounded vicious. We were moving fast, and it seemed like it was coming right behind us, following us out. That's the first time I was ever real glad to be getting out of there, not 'cause I was tired, or I'd found some new place and wanted to tell about it, but 'cause I was just plain scared."

"No wonder those men were so quiet while they were eating," I said. "What do you think was making those sounds if it wasn't spirits?"

"Now that I have time to think on it, it must have been Venture. With the echoes and all in there, it'd be pretty easy to make some strange noises. Sound, it's tricky in there. Sometimes I can hear Echo River when I'm a long way from it, and other times I don't hear it at all till I come round a corner and I'm almost in it. Venture must have heard us coming, or seen the lantern light, or something like that, and set up a racket to protect her and Primmy." He held up his hand to keep me from starting to talk. "Those men want Venture back in the worst way. And that baby, too."

"So they're not leavin'?" Mittie asked, getting right to business while I was still being glad they hadn't found Venture and Primmy.

"Nope. They're convinced those two are in there. But they

don't want to go back in, so they're going to park those dogs right at the entrance to the cave and keep them there till Venture comes out, even if it takes weeks."

"But she has to come out!" I said, close to crying. "She has to get free."

"Well, she can't come out this way."

"But you said . . . don't you think there's another way out? One far away from here? You can take her out that way. You said you would."

"I told her that to calm her down. What I said was I *think* there's another way out. I mean, I'm sure it's there, I've just never gone all the way on it. I don't know how long it takes, or how hard, or if—"

"But you've got to get them out, and that's the only way." Tears were on my face now, and Mittie was hushing me, and she was right. I was getting too loud.

"I can try," he said, taking hold of both my hands. "I've already asked Mr. Miller if I can go back in to keep looking, to find out if she's in there or not, while the dogs are waiting outside. He said that was fine, to take as long as I need to. And he told me to take you with me, to manage the baby if I have to drag Venture out. He says he can spare you for a day or so."

I had to shake my head. "He really thinks I could stand by, holding a baby screaming for her mama while you dragged her out."

"All he's thinking about is this cave. He wants to know for sure if she's in there or not, so those two and their dogs can get out of here either with her or to keep looking for her. They're bad for business, all sour-faced and ill-humored the way they are. Sometimes Mr. Miller forgets I'm somebody who might be thinking about something besides the cave."

"You should be glad of that," I said. "That means he's not thinking you'll be helping a runner."

"True," he said. "And I *am* glad of it."

Then Mittie and Stephen were both talking at once. Mittie was saying, "You want to get all four of you dead, goin' somewhere you don't know where you goin'?" and Stephen was saying, "I have to try. But I can't promise for certain I can do it."

I had to put my hands over my ears. And then I said, "I'm not just coming with you. I'm running, too. With Venture and Primmy. If we start now, maybe we'll be out by morning."

Then both Stephen and Mittie were silent.

"I mean it," I said. "I'm ready to go. I'm being sent off to Louisville for the winter anyway. Who knows if I'll ever get to come back here?"

Well, now I'd done it. I could hardly believe those words came out of my own mouth. But I needed so much to know that baby would be able to grow up free. I was going to make sure it happened.

25

STEPHEN LOOKED AT ME A LONG, LONG TIME. AND then he said, "If that's what you want. I'll tell Mr. Miller you had an accident in the cave. A fatal one. And you fell into such a deep hole I couldn't get your body out. Go get your things." And he turned his face away from me. I'd heard about having your heart broken, but I never thought that was true. I knew about having a pain in your heart that stayed and stayed. Like when Mama and Sally and the boys got sold away. That came on fast and never left. But breaking—that's different. Sudden and sharp. After Stephen turned his face from me, I knew you can truly feel it when it happens.

There wasn't much to put in my bundle, but I went and did it, and came back to the kitchen house in the dark, my heart with the crack in it beating hard and fast. Mittie gave me one tight hug, and then went off to her cabin. She'd said enough goodbyes in her lifetime to not want to linger over new ones.

Stephen's face was set like stone when he and I took up the lanterns, the oil, and the sacks of food Mittie had fixed.

"Once we get out, do you know where we're supposed to go?" I had to ask.

"Mittie told me. I'll make sure you and Venture know."

We went down to the entrance of the cave, dodging through the shadows, with me shivering all the way. It wasn't so cold out, but I was more scared of going in that cave than I had been the first time I'd done it. That time I trusted Stephen to get me out. I still trusted him, but this time I wasn't sure he *could* get me out. Or what I'd be coming out to. And I was scared of the dogs, and of getting caught. I was tired of being so scared. I wanted to leave it all behind me.

The dogs were there, at the cave opening, their lead ropes tied to a tree. They were lying down, but their noses were still working. When we came by them, they made little noises in their throats, but they didn't get up. We weren't what they were waiting for. Not then, anyway.

We didn't talk, going in. I wanted Stephen to try to change my mind so I'd know it mattered to him if I left, but he kept quiet, just moving along at a good clip, dropping lots of Mittie's red pepper behind us just in case Jack and Harlan decided to take the dogs in with Nick and Mat.

We found Venture nursing Primmy and singing to her real soft. It was a sweet picture, one I hated to interrupt. But we had to get going.

Stephen explained about Jack and Harlan, and the dogs, and how we had to go out another way.

"Sounds funny to say," Venture said, getting ready, "but I'll be missing this place. First time ever in my life I had nothing I had to do except rest and be with my little baby. I got to say, I liked that a whole lot, even with the dark and the strange sounds. You hear any of that screamin' earlier? It turned my blood cold. And then it stopped. Just stopped like it was turned off. And then it came again, but different, more low and mean. Yet I wasn't scared. Somehow I knew those sounds wasn't meant for me."

"I heard them," Stephen said. "I thought it might have been you making them."

"Me?" She laughed a little. "You think I know how to make noises like that? Not in a hundred years."

I had to hold my tongue hard to keep from saying to Stephen, "See? I told you." But I kept myself quiet. I wanted to see what Stephen would say to Venture now.

"Well, whatever it was, we've still got to get ourselves out of here. As long as you're sure those sounds aren't meant for us."

He was trying to make a joke of it, but I saw he had something new to think about.

"Charlotte's comin', too?" Venture asked, tying Primmy to her with the shawl Mittie had given her so she'd have her hands free to help us carry the lanterns, oil, and food.

Stephen didn't say anything. He was leaving this one to me.

"I'm coming along with you," I said, holding up my little bundle for her to see.

"That's good," Venture said. "Goin' alone can get awful scary."

"We've got some scary places to go yet," Stephen said. "We're going to have to go out that new way. It's a way I know is there, but I've never gone clear to the end of it, so I don't know how hard it is."

Venture straightened up her back. "I've had a long hard trip already. I can go some more."

I wished I could be as brave and sure as Venture. She knew she had to run 'cause she had the world's best reason: Primmy. My reasons were still soft, and halfway wrong. Most likely Stephen was right. We were as good as free where we already were, where there were no whippings, and I could read and write, and I had a room all to myself.

Maybe real freedom wasn't any better. Maybe even harder. Maybe just as scary. I knew what I already knew, but I didn't know how freedom was. I'd have to want something I didn't know about awful bad to do what I was doing. I thought I wanted it, but there was something—someone—else I wanted, too. And I couldn't have both.

"We need to get started," Stephen said, handing us each a lantern and a sack of food.

We took off walking after him. Along the way we passed by the beautiful Charlotte's Grotto and had to stop a minute for Venture to look, and to catch her breath since we were moving pretty fast. She was just plain amazed, and I was, too, all over again. I bet there wasn't any other place in the whole world like that one. Stephen looked at me, like he was reminding me of my first time in the cave, and of coming to see this with him, but he didn't say one word.

Then we were moving on again, and it was hard. We had falls of rocks to climb over, and little narrow squeezy places to get through—so squeezy Venture had to take Primmy off her chest and hand her on to Stephen so she could fit. We went down steep places and up steep places, and sometimes we walked in water.

Then there were times Stephen left us, to go see where some passage went, or to try to find an easier way. And I had to worry that maybe he wouldn't come back, and there was too much not said between us. The whole time, I was thinking about how much farther I was getting from everything I knew and understood—and I wasn't sure I was getting closer to something better.

When we'd stop to rest, we'd eat a little, and Venture would feed her baby. Primmy was so good, hardly ever made a peep as long as she could stay close to her mama. It made my heart sore for every little one who didn't get to have that, too.

Stephen was quiet, concentrating hard. I got some notion then of how he was when he was exploring, with no others to worry about. And I got some notion, too, of how hard what he did was. I never had seen a place so strange and so big and so perilous as that cave. There was nothing I wanted more than to just get out of there fast as I could. I kept thinking how far down under the ground we were, in the dark, in places where nobody had been before us. Places nobody on top could even imagine, and where nobody would know to look for us if something bad happened and we couldn't get out.

I had to take a lot of deep breaths to keep myself from making some of those screaming noises Stephen and Venture had heard. I couldn't even ask Stephen if he was sure he was going in the right direction. I saw him looking at his little compass from his pocket, but how much help that is when you're down under so much dirt and rocks, and so twisted and turned and upped and downed, I couldn't say.

But we kept on. I didn't know what time it was, or how long we'd been at it, or how close we were to getting to the end. I just kept putting one foot down and then the other, or helping Venture through something, or over something, or holding Primmy while we rested, even sleeping some, too.

We added oil to the lamps, so I knew we'd been going at least ten hours 'cause Stephen had told me the lamps could burn that long on one filling. I was starting to think I didn't need to worry about any freedom since I'd never be getting to it, even if the underground railroad I was on really was underground.

And then we saw light ahead. We'd been so long in the dark, with just our lantern light, at first I couldn't think what it was. Stephen stopped us.

"Stay here," he said. "I'll look."

Venture and I were glad to sit. Even when Stephen went off with his lantern, the light stayed ahead of us just the same.

"You think that's outside?" Venture asked. "You think we're there?"

"Looks that way. Stephen'll tell us what to do next." I still had trust in him. Look how far he'd brought us in an unknown place— and I still wanted to be where he was. Because I loved him. But I also wanted for him to tell me he wanted me to be with him.

Maybe pride can make you stupid, but that's how I was. He had to say it first or I was going on with Venture to somewhere I wasn't sure I wanted to be.

After a while Stephen came back, and his lantern was out. He was walking like a person mighty pleased with himself, and he had a great big smile on his face. He didn't even have to tell us we were there. We knew.

Right then I wasn't thinking about what could happen next. I was just so glad to be getting where I could be on the outside again. But I did consider how Stephen could go back so much faster than he came without Venture and Primmy and me slowing him down.

We followed Stephen up a long slope with the light from the outside coming on brighter and brighter, until we were at the cave mouth and could see the sun, way up in the sky, sending out rays through the trees like the pictures in Mama's Bible, welcoming us back into the world.

26

Stephen made us stay inside a little ways but not so far that we couldn't see the daylight from outside, and we sat on some rocks while he gave us Mittie's directions for how to get to the Ohio River and across. They were kind of fuzzy directions, since she hadn't been sure where we were going to come up, but I figured Venture had been operating on even fuzzier ones so far, and look how far she'd gotten.

"You should stay in here until it gets dark," Stephen told us. "You'll do better traveling at night, especially the closer you get to the river. Find a safe place and sleep in the day."

Venture was nodding, but she probably could have been giving lessons on escaping to Stephen, who didn't know any more about it than I did. Venture was the expert there.

"It'll be easier now," Venture said, "since I know we're close. And I got food. And a warm shawl. Lots easier."

"You and Primmy, you'll do fine," Stephen said. "That little baby's going to have the best present she can have—her mama with her while she grows up." Then he turned to me. "You ready?"

I couldn't say I was. But I didn't want to say I wasn't. So I just stayed quiet.

Venture got up and moved a little way off to feed Primmy. She wasn't paying any attention to me and Stephen.

He asked me again. "You ready?"

"I don't know," I said, real soft.

"It's a hard thing. But you told me you want it."

I was quiet some more.

"If you're not ready, you'd better tell me now."

I looked out through the cave mouth and knew that beyond it was a new place, a place on the way to being free . . . or being caught. I couldn't forget that could happen, too. Just 'cause I was thinking about running didn't mean I'd be getting away.

Seemed like these were things I should have thought about before I got this far. And I had, but they never seemed as real as they did right then.

"I'm not sure," I finally could whisper to him.

"You don't have a lot of time to decide," he said. "I need to start back. Is there something I can do to help?"

I nodded, but I couldn't look up at him. I just kept a close eye on my shoes.

"What?"

Venture went on murmuring to Primmy. She might have figured something was going on with me and Stephen, but she was staying out of it. She had her own things to worry about; she sure didn't need any of mine.

"You can say something," I told him.

He took a big deep breath. "I've said plenty already. You know how bad I feel. About you. About you running. What else can I say now?"

I was quiet some more. Mostly 'cause I didn't know what else to say, either. But also I knew that sometimes, if a body stays quiet long enough, the other person keeps talking. There's something about quiet that makes you want to fill it up.

"You want me to beg you?" he said. "I can do that. But I'm not looking to get my feelings, my heart, you know, kicked in. I told you my feelings. I thought you felt the same way. I guess you weren't as sure as I am about us."

My eyes filled up with tears, and there came such a big lump in my throat I couldn't have talked even if I'd known what I wanted to say. All I could do was kind of bob my head up and down.

He kneeled down in front of where I was sitting, and took hold of both my hands. "What do you want?" he asked me.

Well, that was the question, wasn't it? Now I was just shaking my head.

"You know, if you keep sitting here while Venture leaves, you've made a choice without saying one word. What makes you want to stay?" he asked.

I squeezed his hands.

"I want that, too," he said. "We can have it."

Tears kept coming out of my eyes like rain pouring down.

"What makes you want to go?"

I was shaking my head again. Right then I didn't want to go. Anywhere. I didn't want to go on with Venture, and I didn't want to go all that way back through the dark, and the hard places. I just wanted to sit where I was, and let the whole messy world go roaring on without me. I was just me, just an unimportant person, somebody to carry trays and empty chamber pots, somebody with work-raw hands and a tired, skinny body. Why was I having to make such a big choice? I, the real me inside, didn't matter to anybody.

Anybody but Stephen.

I stood up then, not letting go of his hands. I would have to be going back through those hard dark places, after all. I had plenty of courage to help others run, but not enough to go, too. Only enough to stay.

Venture had finished feeding Primmy, who was all sleepy now and tied into her mama's shawl. Venture wasn't saying anything, but I could see she was getting jittery, wanting to know if I'd be going with her or not.

I sniffed real hard to see if I could quit crying, but it didn't work. I was just going to have to keep crying while I said goodbye to Venture and Primmy. I'd already said goodbye to a lot of people I didn't want to leave, so this was new. I was sad to see them go, but this time I *did* want them to leave.

I hugged Venture hard, kind of squashing Primmy between us. But she was so sleepy she just made a few little squeaks.

"Ain't you coming with us?" she asked me.

"I guess not," I told her. "But I'm real glad I got to come all this way with you and Primmy. I want to see you go on to the North. To be free."

"You think we going to make it?" She held Primmy a little closer.

"I know you will. You didn't come this far to not get there."

"I guess we'll have to go on without you, then," she said. "You know I ain't got enough words to say thank you."

"You've already said it. Now, you and Primmy rest until it gets dark. And take all kinds of care on your way." Tears were still pouring down my face, but I must have been getting used to them 'cause they weren't bothering me anymore. Maybe when there's something you ought to be crying about, well, you *ought* to be crying.

Venture grabbed Stephen's hands with both of hers and shook them real hard. "Primmy and me, we're going to lie down over there and sleep till it's time to go. You all take care going back." She tucked herself and Primmy behind a pile of rocks and was gone from our sight.

I thought I'd cried all I could already, but I was wrong.

That's when Stephen put his arms around me and just held on to me while I bawled. It wasn't only Venture and Primmy I was crying about, but so many other losses and sadnesses. And some glad things, too, like finally being sure about Stephen, and having an owner who didn't whip, and then being so tired, and having to go back inside that cave, and—oh, such a lot of things. I was feeling raw inside, and outside as well, that's all.

I don't know how long we stood there, but after a while Stephen said, "We can rest a little, and then we have to start. We've been away a long time already, and we have a long way to go back."

We went farther inside the cave and sat down, leaning against the wall. It felt like something inside my chest had knitted itself back together, and that sharp painful feeling in there stopped. Then I was asleep in a minute, like I was falling into a long, dark hole. Seemed like I was down there only a minute until Stephen was shaking me awake.

"Sorry," he said. "I hate to be waking you up, but we need to get going. You ready?"

I found out I was a lot readier to go back with Stephen than I was to go on with Venture. There I was, giving up on freedom, and taking a chance on the life I had so I could keep Stephen in it, which was by no means a sure thing. Sometimes thinking isn't enough. Feeling counts, too.

We went back hard and hungry 'cause we'd given all the food to Venture. I thought we'd be going faster, but it seemed slower, like we were going to be in that cave forever. All I could do was follow Stephen, crawling up and down and through, sometimes squeezing, sometimes helping him up, sometimes resting, not thinking, just keeping going.

And then we went by Charlotte's Grotto. I was so surprised I made a sound.

Stephen laughed. "So. You know where we are."

"Thank the Lord. We're almost there."

"Be good if we knew what we'd be coming out to."

"You think those dogs'll still be there?"

"I don't doubt it. I'm just hoping they won't smell Venture on us."

"We've been walking in water, crawling through mud, and sweating like pigs. They're going to take one sniff of us and turn tail running."

And then we were laughing like we'd lost our minds. We laughed so hard we had to sit down, hanging on to each other, with tears coming down our cheeks. We were gasping for breath, and starting up again laughing when we thought we were finished. Maybe we were glad to be safe and back, or we were too tired to be making good sense, or maybe we were a little crazy by then. Anyway, it felt good to be together, and laughing, since we didn't know what waited outside for us.

And while we laughed, it seemed to me I could hear other laughing besides ours. Far away and faint, but not our own laughing. I knew I wouldn't say anything to Stephen about it. He'd tell me it was my imaginings, or an echo, or some such. But I liked thinking those cave spirits were glad for us, glad we'd found ourselves something to be so happy about while they were still searching.

I promised myself that if it seemed like Dr. Croghan was going to sell me, or keep me in Louisville, I really would run. And if I did, Stephen would have to come with me. I wasn't going through everything I had just to end up being apart from him for longer than a winter in Louisville.

All that was ahead. Then we were laughing again, and getting ready to come out of the cave into the rest of our hard life together.

Author's Note

Underground is a novel, not a biography. What I have done, in effect, is invented an alternate universe using Mammoth Cave and people who actually lived there as components of it, but giving the people different personalities, and having different events occur in a different chronology.

While Stephen Bishop was a real person, a slave and a guide in Mammoth Cave, most of the events in this book are completely imaginary. Stephen did become widely known as a result of his explorations in the cave (though the reporter Blair Fleming and his paper the *Ledger-Dispatch* are fictitious), and he did find many exciting geologic wonders. He was the first to cross Bottomless Pit, and the first to find an underground river. He did draw a map that was published and used as the definitive cave guide for many years. But I have taken great liberties with the chronology of those events, and also with the geography of the cave.

Stephen did fall in love with the real Charlotte Brown, he worked with the real Mat and Nick Bransford, he was owned by the real Franklin Gorin and Dr. John Croghan, and Archibald Miller, Jr., actually managed the cave.

However, the personalities of all these real people are totally the products of my imagination, and any perceived misrepresentations have no basis in fact. Furthermore, there is *no* indication that Mammoth Cave ever had any involvement with sheltering runaway slaves, though it is tempting to think that it could have, situated as it is on a direct route between the slave states of the Deep South and the free states across the Ohio River.

Although Stephen was able to read and write, which was unusual for a slave, he left no written record—no diary or letters; nothing but his name, and Charlotte's, scratched or smoked onto the walls and ceilings in many places in Mammoth Cave. All that is known of him comes from contemporaneous newspaper stories, letters written by, and interviews with, his owners and tourists whom he guided.

Franklin Gorin summed him up: "The celebrated and great Stephen . . . was a self-educated man. He had a fine genius, a great fund of wit and humor, some little knowledge of Latin and Greek, and much knowledge of geology, but his great talent was a knowledge of man."

This kind of praise for a slave in the antebellum south was extraordinary.

Stephen Bishop stayed at Mammoth Cave until the end of his life, which came in 1857, when he was about thirty-six. Dr. Croghan died in 1849 and, true to his word, freed Stephen in his will—but only after seven years had passed. In the will, Stephen was valued at $600 and Charlotte at $450.

During those seven years, Stephen bought property and saved

money to try to buy the freedom of Charlotte (by then his wife, though not legally, since slave marriage was not recognized by the state of Kentucky) and that of their son, Thomas. Stephen was able to enjoy his freedom for only one year before his death. Charlotte, who became the director of the dining room at Mammoth Cave, achieved her own freedom only after the Emancipation Proclamation. For her second husband, she chose Nick Bransford, who saved enough money to purchase his freedom but continued to serve as a guide at the cave for the rest of his life.

Mat Bransford remained a slave until Emancipation, and a guide at Mammoth Cave all his life. He married a slave and had four children, three of whom were sold away.

Stephen is buried at Mammoth Cave. In 1878 Charlotte convinced the Pittsburgh millionaire James R. Mellon, who was visiting Mammoth Cave, to provide a headstone for Stephen's unmarked grave. He did so, though he wrongly noted the year of death as 1859 rather than 1857.

Stephen's curiosity did lead him to speculate that there could be a connection between Mammoth Cave and the Flint Ridge Cave system over three miles away across the Houchins Valley. In 1972 a group of six cavers went underground near Salts Cave on the Flint Ridge side and emerged fourteen hours later in Mammoth Cave, becoming the first people to traverse the link between the two caves.

A few days later, on examining the map of Mammoth Cave that Stephen had drawn, one of those cavers noticed that the route they had followed joined with a passage that Stephen had discovered in his explorations and drawn on his map. The passage, Hanson's Lost River, was dry during Stephen's time, but after the damming of Green River was flooded in all but the most drought-stricken years, making it almost impossible to locate again.

At one point, Stephen told Dr. Croghan that he bet Mammoth Cave extended for over 300 miles. Now, more than 160 years later, the cave measures upward of 350 miles, making it the longest cave in the world, with more yet unexplored.

As for the Underground Railroad, it operated with great secrecy from the end of the eighteenth century until 1861, when the Civil War began. Information about it was passed quietly by word of mouth. Often, a conductor at a station on the Railroad knew only about the next stop and not about any others. Runaways were sometimes guided by marks on trees; by rumor; or perhaps by quilts whose patterns may have contained information, hanging on clotheslines or out of windows, but always by the North Star.